# GILGAMESH

## THE SUMERIAN KING

1

# FOREWORD

The story of Gilgamesh predates any known heroic epic.
From Beowulf to King Arthur; from Odysseus to Hercules, most
known mythologies are thought to have sprung from the story of
Gilgamesh. Most Historians do not dispute the existence of
Gilgamesh as a real ruler of Sumeria sometime around 2700 B.C.,
making him the 4th ruling King after the supposed great flood on
Earth which occurred approximately 3100B.C., 400 years before
Gilgamesh. Many things were written about Gilgamesh starting
about 2000 B.C., on several clay tablets in cuneiform writing. The
actual Sumerian language bears no resemblance to any other
known language today. An epic poem was written about Gilgamesh
by the Akkadians, who conquered the Sumerians several centuries
later. The Sumerian text was integrated into the Akkadian language
on 12 stone tablets. The fullest surviving version, from which the
novel is derived, is taken from those twelve stone tablets, originally
written in the Akkadian language, and found in the ruins of the
library of Ashurbanipal, king of Assyria 669-633 B.C., at Nineveh.
The library was destroyed by the Persians in 612 B.C., and all the
tablets were subsequently damaged in several places. The original
epic also was translated into Hittite and Hurrian around the same
time as the Akkadian version.

Though much has been written academically about
Gilgamesh, he is still one of the littlest talked about or well known
epic heroes in history. His story predates all other known legends or
myths, and I felt it was time that there was a story written about
Gilgamesh which not only chronicles the epic taken from the
tablets, but invites the reader to experience Sumerian culture and
immerse themselves in what might have taken place during the

reign of Gilgamesh from a human aspect that is identifiable to the common human experience.

Though I follow the epic's storyline closely as it was originally written, many of the characters in the following book do not appear in the original epic; rather, they were added to enrich the story's dynamic appeal for the reader. It is, after all, a *fictional* account of the epic, though the storyline mainly follows the original Akkadian tablets.

The original story also uses units of measurement known as cubits and leagues, which were commonly used for many centuries after the time of Gilgamesh. In the story, I have changed the units of measurement to more common units such as feet or meters. I also have included, after each introduction to a new tablet, an old Sumerian Proverb which I feel best sums up the content or meaning of the Tablet.

The story of Gilgamesh may well have been the inspiration for many other mythological stories. There exist within the story many common themes we see repeated in all mythological stories that came much later in history: A powerful ruler who abuses his power is brought down and humbled by the protagonist character, The Antagonist then turning to do good and facing many challenges along the way; in later tablets, the Gods intervening with their human creations and either cursing or blessing them in their quests; the Gods coming down to Earth in human form and seducing humans and bearing children; and the idea of "lesser Gods", or angelic figures whom serve the main Gods, both watching over and judging humans in the end. Many of the themes are repeated in later mythologies of all nations, and may have all been inspired from the Epic of Gilgamesh.

I hope you will enjoy The Epic of Gilgamesh as I have presented it. I have endeavored to make the story rich with deep character interaction and storylines, as well as interesting facts about ancient Sumeria and its culture. We do, after all, learn from the past, and if we can learn anything from the story of Gilgamesh, it is that the human experience never ceases to be a common one, despite language, culture, or geography. The story of Gilgamesh is common to all our fears, aspirations, failures, and triumphs as human beings, as well as the constant growth in wisdom and spirit that we all experience throughout the course of a lifetime!

# TABLET ONE

*"The destruction is from his own personal god; he knows no savior..........."*

An enormous sound, as if a star had fallen from heaven awoke him from his sleep. He lay momentarily there, in his bed, trying to discern what he had just heard. What could have made such a sound as this?

Pulling back his silk sheets, adorned with gold and made of the finest wool and flax in all the land, Gilgamesh arose from his bed. Standing nearly 7 feet in height, the imposing figure walked toward the doorway to his bedroom, stopping only for a moment, as he felt a breeze blow across his neck. There was no open window in his chamber however, at least, not that he knew of. He opened the door of his bedroom and walked down the stairway to the main palace chamber on the first floor.

"Where are all my servants?" he wondered aloud. "Surely they must have heard this sound! What incompetence for my servants to sleep through anything! Even if the palace caught fire, or there were an attack the lazy dogs would probably sleep!"

Running over to the main entrance of the palace, he flung the doors open wildly. He was astonished by what he saw; there before him was an awesome sight. In front of the Palace's main door was an axe lodged into the ground. But this was no ordinary axe; this axe was one to whose size he had never seen before! It was as if someone had picked up the axe and stuck it into the ground right in front of the palace.

"But who could have possibly achieved such a feat?" Gilgamesh muttered to himself. The axe was at least 30 feet high and 60 feet long. Its weight would be more than any dozen men could lift! It both intrigued and concerned Gilgamesh at the same time. He stood beside the axe and looked from side to side, searching for signs of the perpetrator who left this massive gift. Who could have done this, and furthermore, what did it mean? And where were all his servants? Returning inside his palace, Gilgamesh raced to the chamber doors of his servants, but found all of the beds empty. "What is this?!" Gilgamesh yelled, enraged that his servants were nowhere to be found. His bellowing voice only echoed in the silence. "They shall receive a sound thrashing and then death for this outrage!" he roared.

Running back outside to where the axe still stood, Gilgamesh stood for a moment, sizing up the object. He couldn't help but smirk in admiration for whoever had the strength to have left it.

"I will move it," he said proudly out loud. "And whoever has done this will pay for leaving this 'gift' for me, whatever the meaning!"

Gilgamesh was no ordinary man. The people of Uruk had many times witnessed his strength and power; the power of the Gods! Gilgamesh was as strong as 20 men. He had the beauty that no other man had ever dreamed to have in his face, and his body was a chiseled work of perfection. He had greater wisdom and cunning than any of the wisest scholars in all Sumeria. But for the people of Uruk, this was a double-edged sword. His power and wisdom made it impossible for any other kingdom to challenge Uruk; not the Egyptians in the west, the Assyrians in the north, or the Akkadians in the south. But he was also a cruel ruler. Quick to put to death any man, woman, or even child who defied him. His servants served him with trembling in their hearts, as one mistake could cost them their lives. Gilgamesh took any woman that he sought to consume with his lustful pleasure, even if they were married to another. His arrogance and anger were often uncontrollable, and he ruled Uruk and Sumeria with an iron fist!

The mammoth Axe stuck to the ground at an angle, so Gilgamesh crouched beneath the top of the handle and prepared to lift. Gathering all his strength, he thrust his legs upward while putting the base of the axe handle on his shoulders. He struggled for several minutes, but to no avail. Try after try, he attempted to move the axe, before collapsing in exhaustion. Never before was there an object he could not move with his great strength. Gasping to catch his breath, Gilgamesh stared at the axe. Laying flat on his back next to the axe in seeming defeat he let out a great roar of frustration. Why could he not move it? He had never failed before. Laying there for a few moments, pondering his dilemma, Gilgamesh finally sat up. He felt a wave of something he had never felt before. It was an odd feeling; an epiphany of sorts. He suddenly realized that this axe was special. It was meant for him to have. He should not try to lift it up to dispose of it; rather, he should cherish it. The feeling was odd but comforting. It just felt so right. He felt the need to embrace the axe as a man would a wife. After standing a moment to contemplate these strange feelings, Gilgamesh finally decided to take the axe to his mother's Palace and present it to her. She would know what to make of it, Gilgamesh thought to himself.

Gilgamesh rose to his feet and positioned himself under the axe again. Something told him that it would move this time. Sure enough, when Gilgamesh lifted, the axe came off the ground on his shoulders with ease. He took the axe on his shoulders and carried it to the doorstep of his mother's dwelling not far away from the main Palace. She heard him walking up to the door, and opened it just as he reached it. Staring into her son's eyes, she watched as he laid the axe down at her feet.

Just then a great light from above shined on Gilgamesh. His mother spoke to him as he gazed up at the bright, almost blinding light from above.

"You must not embrace this axe my son," his mother warned. Gilgamesh looked back down from the light to his mother's face.

"Why must I not?" he inquired.

"You will compete with this axe for the glory of Uruk," she stated.

"But I have brought the axe to your doorstep, and laid it at your feet for you!" Gilgamesh exclaimed, baffled by his mother's words.

As this was occurring, all of the people of Uruk were coming out from their homes and gathering around Gilgamesh and his axe.

"Look at the size of the axe!" the people exclaimed. "It must surely be a gift from the Gods!" The people all buzzed around the axe and marveled at its size and beauty. Its silver metal shone brightly and its proportions were flawlessly perfect except for its mighty size.

Gilgamesh stared at his mother and exclaimed, "See mother, all of the people of my Kingdom can see the beauty of this axe." His mother turned her face away and repeated herself.

"You will compete with this axe for the glory of your Kingdom my son," she said solemnly. Then slowly she closed the door of her home. Gilgamesh yelled for his mother to stop, but to no avail. He watched it as the door shut closed on him.

Just as the door closed shut, Gilgamesh stirred in his bed. Sitting up, he noticed a bead of sweat rolling down his forehead. The room was completely dark except for the light of the moon shining through the window. He was breathing heavily and his heart raced. Looking around his bedroom chamber, he suddenly realized he had been dreaming. Climbing out of bed, he walked to the window of his bedroom. Standing naked, for he was in too much hurry to cover himself, he stared out the window down toward the entrance to his palace which was to the left of his chamber window. He could see nothing but the ordinary darkness of night. There was no axe, or anything else for that matter. Gilgamesh walked back and sat down at the foot of his bed. What could all of this mean? He had never had such a dream that felt so real. He would have to ask his mother in the morning, as she was all wise in these matters. After all, she had once come from the sky herself.

The next morning Gilgamesh awoke early and went to his mother's Palace, which was just to the east of his own. He had built this Palace for her right after he had taken power in Uruk. It was not as big as his own Palace, but it was certainly as lavish. She had many servants day and night to tend to any whim she had. Many of the servants were handpicked by Gilgamesh's mother herself; most of them young males. Gilgamesh suspected her real motive for this, but never asked. It wasn't his business. Anyway, he could hardly judge her. Not after the collection he had built in his own royal harem. The walls were adorned with Gold and only the finest dates and fruits were picked for her consideration. Each week, the purest and best sheep was selected among the livestock for a feast. His Mother's name was Rimat-Ninsun, but she was more commonly called Nininsina. She was to be treated like a Goddess day and night, for she had given up her immortality to live on the Earth with her Son and help rule Sumeria by his side. It was a fact that she made sure no one ever forgot either! She had lived for eons as the Goddess of fertility, and in her mortal form, she was the vision of beauty. She aged at an almost infinitesimal rate, much slower than any human. Her hair was long and black. It hung halfway down her back and had a luster that all women dreamed of having. Her eyes were a mesmerizing shade of blue, like the ocean, and her figure was that of a perfectly sculpted twenty-something woman, though she was a mother to a thirty year old King.

Sitting down beside his mother in her palace dining chamber, Gilgamesh explained the strange dream to her. Nininsina listened intently as he carefully detailed everything he could remember. His mother could interpret dreams more wisely than any priest or wise-man could. After all, she had first-hand experience with visions, creating a few of her own in her time.

"Well, what do you think?" Gilgamesh inquired after he had finished the tale. His mother stood up and paced the floor a few times before answering, probably just for the drama he guessed.

"The dream you had *is* a future vision my son," she assured him. "There will come from the forest a man; a certain man, and this man will possess more strength and power than you have ever faced in any opponent!"

"Who is this man?!" Gilgamesh demanded, insulted she thought that any man could match him in battle. Nininsina shook her head at her son's arrogant attitude.

"Do you not even know what happens in your own Kingdom my son?" she asked him. Gilgamesh face scrunched up in bewilderment.

"I do not understand Mother," he stated, perplexed by her question. "I give my subjects all they need. There has never been a more powerful ruler, capable of assuring their safety from the Akkadians, Syrians, Egyptians...."

"Yes," his mother interrupted, "but you rule with an iron fist that Sumeria has never seen before since the time of the Great Flood!"

Gilgamesh shrugged his shoulders. "So what?" he declared defiantly.

"The people have called upon the Father of the Gods, Anu, to create a being to challenge you," Nininsina replied.

"Challenge?" he laughed. "Challenge me? I am the perfect ruler! Why would they even ask for such a thing? Furthermore, it is a futile plea. There is no warrior who could ever meet me in battle!"

Nininsina shook her head again and sighed. "Your ego will only lead to your destruction someday my son!" she warned. "I did not give up immortality to watch over and rule with you here on Earth, just to witness someday your defeat and destruction!"

Gilgamesh smiled and put his hand on her shoulder. "Do not worry mother, there is no force on this Earth than can defeat me. Even if this man of the forest is to be sent by the Gods....." Gilgamesh trailed off and turned away from his mother, putting his hand on his chin. "But tell me this, why did I feel in the dream the need to embrace the Axe as if it were a wife?"

"Because the man of the forest is your equal *and* your opposite! And deep inside of you, buried beneath the arrogance you display so proudly, you know that to be King and Ruler is not enough. You were never meant in your destiny to wed, take a wife and be a normal man; But from the time you were conceived, your destiny was to be the most powerful man on the face of the entire Earth. Because of me, you are a God, and the Gods can be smug and arrogant, as I well know; but because of your father, you are also deeply rooted in honor and righteousness. This man will help balance in you the good with the bad; the arrogance with humbleness; he will bring out in you the honorable, righteous man that you were also destined to be. You will love him like a brother, but fight him as your darkest enemy!"

"I don't understand," Gilgamesh said, putting his hands up to his face and sitting down. "Is this man real or not? And if so, are you are saying I should fight this man when we meet, or not?"

Nininsina kissed her son on the cheek and looked into his eyes. "He is very real my son. And I'm saying you don't have a choice. You *must* fight him! Whether you win or lose is irrelevant, for what is born out of the conflict will be worth more than anything you have ever learned or achieved up till now!"

"I don't understand," Gilgamesh repeated.

Nininsina smiled. "You will."

-----------------------------------------------------------------------

The young woman stood at the bank of the mighty Euphrates River. Uruk had the fortune of being right next to one of the two mightiest rivers in the world; the Euphrates, just a few miles to the west. The Tigres, which lied about 200 miles to the east, was much further away. So it was the job, each week, for a caravan of workers from the city to go out west to the Euphrates and draw hundreds of gallons of water from the river to be used in the daily lives of the people of Uruk. On this particular day, Shamhat was feeling restless and uneasy. There was a great unrest lately among the people of Uruk. They had begun to grow weary of Gilgamesh and his heavy-handed approach to ruling. She had overheard many of their conversation in markets and public places. They were praying day and night to the Gods to send relief from his tyranny. It seemed a bit ironic to her that they prayed so hard for relief *from* him, when they had prayed years ago that a man *like* him would come and save them from the Assyrians and Egyptians during the reign of King Dumuzi!

But this unrest among the people was only one of her worries. She had had a disturbing dream the night before, and decided to travel with the men to the river while they performed their task, so she could clear her mind. This was generally forbidden, for women were always a great distraction to the men as they performed their tasks, but she had gone anyway. After all, she *was* the keeper of the great harem of the King. There were dozens of concubines that Gilgamesh could call on any day or night to pleasure himself with, but none that he fancied more than Shamhat. She was not the most beautiful of all the women, but she had piercing green eyes, a curvy figure, incredible charm, and a blazing sexuality that bedazzled him. It was this favor of her that had led to his appointing her keeper of his personal harem in Uruk, in charge of overseeing all of his young concubines. Not only that, but after some time, she had also been put in charge of the other personal servants in the palace. Most of them were none too pleased that she had gotten this appointment. A concubine lording over them; it was ridiculous!

Standing on the bank of the river, a gentle breeze blew her long dark hair into the air. She had never cut it since she was a little girl. It reached all the way to her knees, though she usually kept it up in a tight knot on the top of her head. She wore a long white dress which was customary of the women of her time, made of wool and flax. It covered her from head to toe, except for the left arm and shoulder which were exposed. Men also wore such a garment, but theirs were generally shorter and only came to right above their knees. Being a servant of Gilgamesh directly, hers was made of the finest quality material in the land. She grabbed the bottom of her dress and pulled it up past her knees so she could sit on the river bank without dirtying it.

Sitting quietly as the workers gathered water in stone jars, she pondered the dream she had the night before. It was stranger than anything that she could ever remember. Since she was a little girl, she had always had strange dreams that would often foreshadow an event about to happen. However, this dream was special. She could feel it. Particularly, she had many dreams sent to her from the Goddess Ishtar, who was the Goddess of sexuality. She had become aware of the power of sexuality at a very young age, and had always been obsessed with Ishtar; and she seemed to have won favor with the Goddess also. About 100 miles to the southeast lay the city of Mari, where the Temple of Ishtar was. There were many beautiful priestesses living within the temple walls. They prayed day and night to Ishtar, and they both worshipped and "loved" the men who came to the temple to show their love and passion for the Goddess. In return, the men lavished the priestesses with gifts, and left money and offerings of food for the Goddess. Shamhat had always been mesmerized with the glamour of being a temple priestess, and it was her dream one day to be the High Priestess of the temple. But fate had led her to a position of great standing in a different direction. Being the keeper of the King's harem was a much sought out position by any woman. In these times, prostitution was a normal part of society and accepted by the people; and to be the King's number one concubine, in a sense, was one step removed from being a Queen!

In the dream, she was laying naked in the forest. All the animals of the forest stirred around her, as if they were watching her, but she felt no fear. Then something emerged from the shadows. It was large and powerful like a bear, but she did not know what it was. It came close to her. Her heart beat rapidly and her breaths came quickly in her fear, but she could not move. Something was compelling her to lay there. Then the beast came close and lied on top of her. His face was like that of a man, and his eyes were a blazing red. Her fear turned to excitement as the beast came inside of her and made wild love to her. It was both terrifying and intoxicating. After some time, the beast vanished and she lay there exhausted from the experience. Then she had awoken. This dream was unlike any she had ever had. Was it a vision from Ishtar, she wondered? Shamhat had had many visions of future events that had led her to good fortune in life. It was as though she was favored in Ishtar's eyes and the Goddess saw to her fortune and goodwill. At least, after she had begun following her as a teenager. But this dream was dark and disturbing. If it was of the future, she thought. What could it represent?

The men had finished packing the asses, and Shamhat pulled her hair up and tied it in a tight bun on top of her head. She got up from the bank of the Euphrates and walked over to one of the workers. Walking around him as he eyed her lustfully, she ran her finger up and down his back. The man shuddered in delight and sighed heavily. Shamhat then grinned at the man and walked away. She loved to entice men, only to leave them wanting and unfulfilled! It was a woman's greatest power after all, and her greatest source of control. One day it would lead her to be sitting by the side of her King, she mused to herself. Only then could she wield real power!

When they arrived back in Uruk, Aruru was awaiting her as they came to the entrance to the Great city. There was a massive wall that surrounded the entire city. Gilgamesh had commissioned the building of the wall just after he had retained power in Uruk. The wall stood 20 feet high and was made of dried mud brick, which was extremely hard and durable against attack. Guards, and all of the royal infantry for that matter, wore copper helmets lined with leather for comfort. They were dressed in a cloak armor made of leather for the base and then many metal disks that overlaid the leather to provide protection. They also each held a bronze spear, sword, and something that Gilgamesh's army had recently developed; a bronze socket axe which was most effective in combat for piercing armor of opposing armies.

Most of the houses and shops of the cities were made of this mud brick; it was something that the people of the land had recently begun to do just a century before. Mud brick was much stronger and more durable than the wooden reed houses and buildings the Sumerians had used for centuries before. On the sides of most of the mud brick buildings were magnificent mosaics of painted clay cones. In the old times, the Sumerians had used these pictures as their language, much like the Egyptian Hieroglyphics, but in the last century had developed a new way of writing that was more efficient and intricate called cuneiform; pictographs made entirely out of patterns using an instrument called a stylus that was, essentially, a long piece of wood with a three pronged end in a wedge shape. It had become the standard way of writing. However, the only ones who learned it were the wealthy as it was very difficult to master and took much schooling. Outside the walls of the mighty city, many small wood reed houses still stood. These belonged to the very poor, who could not afford to build the mud brick houses that the wealthier inhabitants inside the walls could afford.

Aruru was a small woman, only standing about 5 feet high, and unlike the rest of the women in Uruk, had cut her hair short to only about the shoulders. All of the other women of the city had looked down on her for her non-conformity, for it was taboo for a woman to cut her hair short; or even a man for that matter. As a matter of practice, the women in Uruk all had long hair that they put up in a bun on top of their head, except for at night when they slept. But Aruru had never been one to follow the rules. It was this aggressive and abrasive personality that had led to her father beating her and leaving her for dead outside of the walls of the city when she was 15. Shamhat happened upon her one day while wandering outside of the wall when she had taken one of her many trips with the workers to the river. Aruru was near death, starved and beaten. She took pity on her and had taken her as her personal servant. Over the next few years, they had grown intimately close, and Aruru had become her most trusted confidant and best friend.

"Where have you been!" cried Aruru in her incomparable raspy voice. Shamhat looked at her, bewildered as to why she was so upset. "Gilgamesh has requested a girl for tonight and he wants her to be ready for him as soon as he is finished with the royal supper!"

"Couldn't you have gotten one of the girls ready? You have been my assistant for many years Aruru," Shamhat complained.

"You know the girls don't respond to me the way they do you," Aruru said, shaking her head.

"Can't imagine why," Shamhat joked. Aruru glared at her, then took the bit of the horse Shamhat was riding to lead her back to the royal brothel where all the girls were housed. Being the head of the Harem for Gilgamesh, Shamhat was housed in the Palace with the King and all of the other personal servants. The Harem where the girls were housed was just outside of the palace. It was a small mud brick house with two levels. At least, it was small in comparison with the Palace. But in comparison to many other shops and houses in Uruk, it was still quite big. It housed about 30 different girls, all handpicked from the town by Gilgamesh himself. They were to be only the most beautiful and young girls for the King's consideration, and only between the ages of 15 and 18. After a girl had reached 18, Gilgamesh no longer desired her. That was not to say that Gilgamesh did not have other women as well. There were many times he rode through Uruk and spotted a young woman, even a married one, and had his way with her. Whatever women he desired, he would take, and if a husband or father of the girl objected, they were immediately slaughtered, along with all of the girl's family, and their house burned to the ground!

Shamhat and Aruru arrived at the harem and tied up the horse outside to a wooden post. Going inside, Shamhat found all of the girls sitting on their knees, laughing and gossiping about whatever they had heard that day from the townspeople. It was their only entertainment. Shamhat stood over them and they immediately were silenced.

"The King wants a girl for tonight," she informed them. "Now who shall it be?" The girls all looked at each other and then back at Shamhat.

"No volunteers?" Aruru said, smirking. "Come on now girls, it is an honor to be the whore of the King tonight!"

"Knock it off," Shamhat said to Aruru, then turned her attention back toward the girls. "Well, if none of you will volunteer, then I shall have to pick one!" The girls let out a groan. None of them wanted to be the one picked. They were all very familiar with the sexual roughness exhibited by Gilgamesh. He was sadistic and cruel. He loved to torture the women, beat them, and hurt them; for him it was an exciting rush. Many of the girls came back bruised and scarred. Gilgamesh regarded women as nothing more than objects to be used in daily life, like cattle, and he openly professed this belief without shame.

Looking over the girls, Shamhat fixed her gaze on one in particular. She was trying to hide in the back behind the other girls. Her name was Siduri. She was 16 and had just recently been picked by Gilgamesh on his latest exploits into the city. Her father was a blacksmith named Dagon. He was the major proprietor of weapons for the royal army and regarded as the finest craftsman in all of Sumeria. Gilgamesh had taken his daughter over his fierce objections, yet Gilgamesh had spared Dagon's life only because of his continued usefulness. Dagon had a knack for creating weapons, including the socket axe, that gave Gilgamesh's army tactical advantages. That, plus the fact that the weapons themselves were never prone to breaking during battle because of the way they were forged; a secret that only Dagon knew and would never reveal. Dagon knew this would keep him alive for many years to come if the royal army wanted his weapons to continue to dominate in battle.

Siduri was perhaps the most beautiful of all the courtesans. She had many suitors before being taken by Gilgamesh. All of the men in the city wanted her for their wife because of her stunning beauty and lilting voice that sounded like an angel. Siduri was tall, nearly 6 feet; this made her taller than some of the men. Yet her face was smooth and flawless and her body was perfect beyond compare with any of the other women in Uruk. She had long dark hair with a tint of red in it. Her eyes were a deep blue, like the ocean. It was very unusual for a Sumerian girl to have deep blue eyes. Usually they were commonly dark brown or black. Shamhat had green eyes which were unusual enough, but to have blue eyes was extremely rare, and it made Siduri's beauty stand out even more. Secretly, Shamhat hated Siduri. Gilgamesh had been unusually delighted with finding her and it drove Shamhat's jealousy to the point of madness. She wanted no other women to have the same favor as she did in his eyes!

"You," Shamhat said, pointing to Siduri. "Come with me!" The other girls looked on with compassion in their eyes as Siduri stepped forward and followed Shamhat out the doorway.

"That precious little thing won't survive the night," Aruru snickered.

---

To the northeast of Sumeria was a breathtaking forest. It lay between the Taurus and Zagros mountains, on the banks of the Caspian Sea. It was thick and dense, and no man could tame it for civilized land. However, there were several trappers that came to the banks of the Caspian Sea to fish, for the fish in the Caspian Sea were far more exotic tasting than those from the Tigres or Euphrates Rivers. These trappers lived near the Zagros Mountains, well isolated from the major Sumerian cities that lined the two mighty rivers. Every few weeks they would venture out to fish and also to set traps at the edge of the forest where the trees weren't as dense. They often caught small rabbits and other small prey that they could take home and feast on as a change from the fish they caught and ate daily.

One day a young trapper named Agga was walking at the edge of the forest, checking the traps that he and his father had set a few days before.

"That's strange," Agga muttered to himself as he walked along, inspecting the traps. All of the traps that he and his father had set had been sprung, but there were no prey inside. It looked as if the animals had wandered in and been trapped as usual, but that someone had set them free. Who could have done this, Agga wondered aloud? All of the trappers were very competitive, but they also had respect for one another; a kind of trappers' code. One trapper would never steal a kill from another. Agga ran off to find his father Adad.

"Father!" Agga cried as he ran towards him at the bank of the sea. Adad, whose flowing white beard touched the sand as he was crouched down, stoop up as his son came running towards him. He had been busy cleaning one of the fish he had just caught by slicing open the belly to disembowel it.

"What is it my son?" Adad asked, dropping his knife to his side. Agga came barreling in and stopped just short of where his father was standing. He was out of breath, and put his hand on Adad's shoulder as he gasped for air to speak. "What on earth are you yelling about?!" Adad demanded.

"Someone has set the animals free!" Agga wheezed. Adad's face scrunched up in confusion.

"What do you mean the animals are free?" he inquired.

"The traps have been sprung, but there is no catch inside! Someone must have set the animals free after the traps sprung father!" Agga said excitedly. Adad shook his head in bewilderment.

"That doesn't make any sense," he said to his son. He walked a few paces away then turned back to him. "Are you quite sure that the traps were sprung?"

"YES, father!" he replied sarcastically. "I have been trapping with you long enough to know when the traps have been sprung!"

"Alright, alright," Adad said, putting his hand up. He walked around on the beach stroking his beard and trying to make some sense of it. If someone had set the animals free, who could it possibly be? For that matter, he had been fishing at the edge of the ocean all day long which was right in front of the entrance to the forest, and not more than 100 yards away. The forest was much too dense to be entered at any other point than this one, so how could any person have sneaked past him and his son without their knowing, and release the animals? It just didn't make sense.

"Come on, let's go," Adad told his son, as he gathered his fishing pole and supplies.

"But what about the traps father?" Agga asked his father. "Should we not find out who has done this?!" Adad shook his head and walked away, carrying his pole. Agga, frustrated by his father's seemingly unconcerned attitude, muttered to himself as he followed behind him. Adad walked for a few steps and then stopped dead in his tracks.

"Did you just hear something?" he asked his son. Agga lifted his head and listened intently to the sounds around him, but heard nothing. He shook his head as his father continued to listen. "There is something moving in that tree over there," Adad said, pointing to a large tree just at the edge of the forest. Agga squinted and looked up at the tree, but saw nothing unusual.

"Are you sure there is something there father," Agga quipped. "I don't see or hear a thing!"

Adad walked a few paces closer to the tree then stopped. Pointing excitedly he shouted, "there, did you see that?!" Agga looked at the top of the tree and saw that some of the branches were moving about, yet there was no sign of any wind. Also, only the top of the tree was moving, while all of the branches near the middle and bottom were completely still.

"It must be some kind of animal," Agga commented, a bit confused. Adad shook his head.

"There isn't an animal alive that I know of that can climb that far up a tree!" Adad exclaimed.

"Maybe it's some kind of bird?" Agga guessed. Again, Adad shook his head.

"No," he began, "it has to be something quite large and strong to shake the entire top of the tree in this manner! Something the size of a lion!" Agga looked at his father as if he were crazy.

"There's no way a lion, or bear, or anything of that size could climb a tree of 100 feet in height without falling father," Agga said. "Maybe it's some kind of large bird or something. You know father, there probably are many kinds of birds and animals that live deep in the forest that we have never seen."

"Perhaps, Adad conceded, "but…..". Adad's thought trailed off as he stared at the top of the tree.

"Come on father, let's go. We can set some new traps tomorrow and see what happens. Maybe we can catch the man who is stealing our dinner!" Agga said, grabbing his father's arm and motioning for him to follow. Adad began walking with his son, keeping a close eye on the tree as they walked to where their asses were waiting. Agga and Adad untied the donkeys and rode them off toward home, all the while Adad was keeping a keen eye back on the tree he had seen moving. It mocked him with its stillness. Adad shook his head and sighed; perhaps he was getting old.

---------------------------------------------------------------------------

Siduri sat in the huge bathtub, reserved for the royal courtesans, as she prepared for her night with Gilgamesh. Three low level servant girls bathed her body and painted her face with colors that were made from white lead and vermilion. These cakes of paint were stored in seashells and applied with small brushes. Gilgamesh loved to have his courtesans fully painted and perfumed before they were to appear before him, and in fact, he himself also loved to paint his face and perfume his body. Despite his utter masculinity, Gilgamesh often displayed the vanity of a woman.

Shamhat stood by in the distance, twirling her long dark hair in her fingers and glaring at Siduri. She didn't know why she had chosen her to be with Gilgamesh that night. At first she thought it would be funny, seeing as how most of the concubines came back with "battle scars". But the more she thought about it now, the more she grew jealous. Part of her wanted to kill Siduri right now in this moment, so she could never spend the night with Gilgamesh; but part of her wanted to please the King and curry his favor as well, and she knew how much Gilgamesh had been looking forward to being with Siduri since he had chosen her. Still, it made her blood boil uncontrollably whenever she thought of the two of them together!

Shamhat knew that none of these women meant anything to Gilgamesh. They were simply there for his amusement and pleasure. But if she could only somehow convince him of the value of taking a Queen to be by his side, she thought to herself. She coveted power more than anything in the world; she wanted to be sitting by the side of the mightiest King ever known and wield ultimate power over her subjects. She could have that power someday, she thought; yes, and even eventually bear an heir, and be the mother of a ruler with the blood of the Gods in his veins. He would be even more powerful than Gilgamesh himself, she mused. The mere thought of these things gave her goose bumps!

After the servant girls had finished with Siduri, Shamhat motioned for her to follow her to Gilgamesh's quarters. Siduri's heart was pounding. She had heard the stories from the other girls that had returned after a night with the King, and was more than a little scared at what would happen; especially because she was a virgin. It was well known that Gilgamesh was even more strong-handed and harsh with the women that no man had ever touched before. He liked to test them and see how far he could go with them before they would break! Pain turned Gilgamesh on. He got a thrill from inflicting pain on the girls while he was with them.

"Would you like a little advice young one?" Shamhat asked Siduri as they quietly neared Gilgamesh's chamber. Siduri nodded nervously.

"When the King is on top of you, do not move, even the slightest little bit," said Shamhat, with a Cheshire cat smile. Siduri stared at Shamhat for a moment, still wrought with fear, then nodded weakly. She was trembling and almost hyperventilating. Shamhat turned around and led Siduri to the chamber door, chuckling to herself all the while. She was thoroughly enjoying the young one's anxiety and fear. Actually, the advice she had given Siduri was meant to infuriate Gilgamesh as she was well aware from her many nights with him that he hated for his concubines to play dead. They were to keep the facade that they loved everything he was doing to them, no matter how painful. Shamhat was sure that when Siduri took her advice that Gilgamesh would be insulted and rip her to shreds! It would be so delicious, she thought, grinning from ear to ear. Just what the little whore deserved for stealing her spotlight!

Shamhat opened the chamber door and motioned for Siduri to enter. Siduri slowly crept into the room with tiny baby steps, looking all around, not quite knowing what to expect. Gilgamesh's chamber room was the most glamorous thing she had ever seen. The bed frame was made of solid gold, as well as all the tiles of the floor. The drapes surrounding the royal bed were also golden in color, and made of the finest silk she had ever seen. All around the room were small marble statues of the Sumerian Gods, including one of his Mother, Nininsina. This one happened to be the largest. Also, the size of the room was something she had never witnessed. This one bedroom in the palace was bigger than the housing quarters for all of the concubines in the harem. It was truly splendid.

As Siduri took in the splendor of the room around her, she momentarily forgot about what was about to take place when The King arrived for her. Shamhat stood by the open door and shook her head, snickering to herself. "Oh how easily distracted and naïve the young ones are," she laughed to herself, and slowly closed the door. She left Siduri to what was sure to be a night she would never forget!

---------------------------------------------------------------------------

Gilgamesh stood up on a large dune that was directly south of his palace. He liked to stand there each night and watch the sun go down in the distance. It was a reminder to him that the cycle of life was much like the cycles of day and night. There was a time of prosperity and daylight, and also a time of night and darkness. He knew that having a mortal father denied him the right of immortality, and this fact had always been in the back of his mind as he ruled over all of Sumeria. His Kingdom had been the richest and most productive of all societies since the great flood nearly five centuries ago, when all of mankind had been thrown into chaos. The flood destroyed all of the earth except for a scattered few chosen by Anu, the King of the Gods, to survive and rebuild, or so the legend went. Gilgamesh never was much interested in history, only the here and now. And in the here and now he was the most powerful man in the world!

But yet, the words his mother had spoken to him earlier in the day had been burning in his memory. Rarely had she ever contradicted him, nor told him he was lacking in anything. If anything, Nininsina had lavished him with praise and affection all of his life. He was always told he would achieve great things; he knew that he would rule all of Sumeria since he was a child, so his mother took great care to prepare him for that very task. She said she had foreseen it ages ago, when she still dwelled in the sky with the other Gods and Goddesses. But yet, this very day, she had chastised him and told him of a man who would be every bit as great as he was! That he needed this man, no less! It gnawed away at his insides that his beloved mother had said these things. But at the same time, his mother was ancient and wise. He knew she could very well be right. Was the dream he saw a vision from Enki and Enlil, the Gods of the Earth and sky? Nininsina had told him that Enki and Enlil had always watched over all of the Kings before him and had given them all special wisdom and knowledge. It was their duty set forth by Anu. But up to this moment the Gods had never personally spoken to Gilgamesh in any form; vision or otherwise!

As Gilgamesh stood and watched the amber sky turn to a deep reddish hue as the sun set over his Kingdom, Shullat came plodding up the dune to where he was standing. Shullat was Gilgamesh's most trusted general. A short man, indeed, but built like an ox in every other respect! He was the strongest warrior in Gilgamesh's army, and his most trusted one as well.

"My Lord," Shullat yelled to Gilgamesh. He turned and glanced at Shullat for a moment, then turned back to stare at the sunset. "My Lord," Shullat continued, "Shamhat has informed me that your......selection for tonight, is awaiting you in your royal chamber." Gilgamesh did not seem to pay any attention to Shullat. Shullat stepped closer to his King and began again. "My Lord....."

"I heard you the first time General," Gilgamesh directed him. He let out a sigh and continued to watch the sunset in silence.

"Do you not wish to go and be with her now Lord?" Shullat inquired. Gilgamesh turned his head toward Shullat and proclaimed, "She *is* my property, and she shall wait for me as long as is necessary."

"Of course my Lord," Shullat replied, kneeling before him. He turned to leave and return to the Palace.

"Shullat...," Gilgamesh began.

"Yes Lord?" Shullat asked, stopping in his tracks.

"Have there been any reports of anything unusual from the forest near the Caspian Sea?"

Shullat raised an eyebrow. "We rarely venture out that far," said Shullat. "But I have not heard of anything strange going on in that area. Why do you ask?" Gilgamesh turned toward him and put his hand on his shoulder, shaking his head.

"It is nothing General." Gilgamesh said, slapping his shoulder a few times.

Shullat looked Gilgamesh in the eyes. "You look very disturbed this evening Gilgamesh. Might I be so bold as to ask why?"

Gilgamesh shook his head and turned away from him to look at the sunset in the distance again. He stood silent for a moment, and then turned back to Shullat.

"Do you know who my father was, Shullat?" Gilgamesh asked. Shullat shook his head no. Gilgamesh huffed and turned away again. He sighed heavily for a few moments then began to speak again. "His name was Lugulbanda. At least that's what I've been told. He was a mighty King who lived before the time of the great flood. Supposedly he ruled for 1200 years."

Shullat raised an eyebrow when Gilgamesh said that. "Is that not impossible Lord.....I mean for any mortal man to live for so long?"

"That's was my first question too," Gilgamesh replied, chuckling. "But my mother told me he was no ordinary man. In fact, he was a man of the purest heart and integrity; so much so, that the Gods granted him immortality for his good deeds."

"Sounds like quite the man, your father," Shullat said.

"Yes, he does, doesn't he?" was all Gilgamesh responded, gazing once again at the sunset, now turning a deep purple as the Sun descended behind the horizon of the dunes. "It was even said that he had the ability to speak to the animals. Particularly, he had a talent for speaking to the birds."

"I see," Shullat said, a bit puzzled by the whole conversation. "And can you also speak with birds?"

"No," Gilgamesh replied, shaking his head. Shullat was starting to wonder what this conversation had to do with anything, but he knew better than to say anything to Gilgamesh.

"He was a General for King Enmerker. When Enmerker died, he became the King," said Gilgamesh, glancing at Shullat before gazing back at the horizon. "He ruled for 1200 years, and brought peace and prosperity to all Sumeria; but the immortality that my father was promised because of his righteousness, disappeared when he met my mother. Their acts together were upsetting to Anu, so he took away Lugulbanda's immortality, and condemned him to die!"

"What happened to him?" asked Shullat, now deeply immersed and fascinated by the story.

"Nobody knows," Gilgamesh said, shaking his head slowly. "He disappeared after that. Some have said that he was taken by Enki deep into the forest, sparing him death, and that he has been there ever since under their protection."

"Doesn't your mother know what happened to him?" inquired Shullat.

"I'm sure she does," Gilgamesh answered, shaking his head again. "She won't tell me."

"My Lord," Shullat began, putting his hand on Gilgamesh's shoulder, "The hour is late. Why don't you go and enjoy your prize for the night. After all, you have been looking forward to this one ever since you picked her out."

Gilgamesh looked over at Shullat who was grinning from ear to ear.

"Shamhat has picked Siduri?" Gilgamesh asked with a surprised tone. Shullat nodded. He couldn't help but smile. He could have easily requested Siduri from Shamhat, but had made his desire to be with a girl tonight vague. It was his attempt to see if Shamhat would pick Siduri or not, since he knew that she had been very displeased and jealous when he had taken her from Dagon. Gilgamesh couldn't help but chuckle to himself as he followed Shullat over to the horse he had brought for him. When they arrived, he stopped in his tracks.

"No Shullat," Gilgamesh said, raising his hand. "I would rather walk back to the palace." Shullat looked at him for a moment, and then shrugged his shoulders. He mounted his horse and led the other horse back to the side of the palace where all the horses were tied at night.

Gilgamesh slowly plodded along in the sand, heading back toward what was sure to be a most fulfilling night with his new courtesan. She was incredibly beautiful! But despite this, all he could ponder was what was to come in the days ahead. The ominous words of his mother still hanging in the clouds above him, Gilgamesh let out a groan. He was still quite confused as to why the Gods would send a man to challenge him. There were times, he supposed, when he was harsh with his subjects; cruel even. But he cared for him Kingdom, and it had never prospered so greatly since his reign. He was sure that he was born and destined to be King, yet now it seemed that his subjects resented him. And now the Gods had sent a man to threaten his authority! It didn't make sense. But then again, his mother had told him for many years that the Gods are sometimes irrational. It was part of the reason that she left the heavens to rule with him on Earth. She wanted to be close to him, to guide him. She also loved living the mortal life of indulgence far more than being stuck in the clouds above with bickering Deities!

No matter, Gilgamesh thought to himself. Despite what his mother had said to him, he would never embrace this man as a friend. He would handily defeat him in battle and send a message to the Gods that there was no other man as great as him in all of Sumeria. That he promised!

------------------------------------------------------------------------

Nininsina kneeled by the foot of her bed, hands together, and head bowed. Though she had given up her place in the heavens for her offspring, she was still able to discern the thoughts of the other Gods through meditation. She would sit for hours at a time in her chambers, concentrating and listening very hard to hear their thoughts. It had always been one of her special powers, which had always driven the other Gods to their wits ends, as she often read their intimate thoughts without their knowledge. During her time in the heavens, Anu, the Father of the Gods, who separated the Earth from the sea, had forbidden her from using her powers on the other Gods, as it created a certain chaos. Secretly though, she had always done it.

But Nininsina was not known as the "great cow" of the Gods without good reason. Out of her great knowledge and unique wisdom sprang great fertility, and she was often sought by the other Gods and Goddesses to predict the future through her visions. She had predicted that the hearts of men would be corrupted after their creation; to the point of destruction. She had been the one that persuaded Anu to set the flood upon the world to destroy it, after she was proven right. But she also predicted that she would produce an heir of great power and strength, who would eventually rule over all of Sumeria. Once again she was proven right after her brief encounter with Lugulbanda. She had chosen him because of the purity of his heart, the intelligence of his mind, the compassion of his spirit, and strength of his character. It was the first time she had ever assumed human form to seduce a human, but it was necessary to conceive a King. However, the experience of the flesh was so pleasing to Nininsina that she had decided to give up her role in the heavens, to live on Earth with her Son, over Anu's objections.

Quietly she sat now, meditating in her chambers to try to hear their thoughts. She could hear the faint whispers of their minds, but it was difficult without being close to them as she once was. After trying for several moments, she decided to give up trying to read their thoughts for the moment, and focus on receiving a vision about the future.

Nininsina took a deep breath, and then held out her hands in front of her body. She breathed deeply, as her mind slipped into an almost hypnotic state. Her eyes turned a milky white color as the vision began to surface. It was a man, but it was still very blurry. Focusing harder, Nininsina could see that the man was naked. He was hairy from head to toe, yet was covered with an almost thick fur, like an animal. Bestowed upon him was the power of all the animals of the forest. He had the keen vision of the eagle so he could see for miles away in the thick forest; He had the strong legs and speed of a gazelle, and could sprint exceedingly fast. He had the cunning of a fox, the leaping ability of a lion, and the strength of a elephant. This man knew not the difference between life or death, sorrow or happiness, or the inherent greed of mankind. He was pure, of the earth, and untarnished by the sinful nature of humans. It was this one that had sent to grapple with her son, and he *would* make the mightiest of opponents for Gilgamesh.

As the vision weakened and faded away from her, Nininsina could feel a cold chill run down her spine. Looking down at her arm, she could see the hair standing up on end. She knew that this man posed the greatest threat to her Son that he had ever known, and his arrogance could very well cost him his life. But she also knew that it was a lesson he *must* learn if he was to become the man he was destined to be from the beginning. Nininsina breathed a deep breath as she rose from her meditation state to go and find Gilgamesh. She needed to inform him that the one he dreamed of was very near, and the beginning of his long journey to righteousness was about to begin soon!

A loud crash startled Nininsina as the door to her chamber had been flung open. Quickly turning toward the noise, she saw her standing there with a smirk on her face. It was Shamhat. Nininsina glared back at her. She had always despised Shamhat. She easily could see through the wretched plans of this harlot; how she worshipped her sister, Ishtar, that most treacherous Goddess of sex, lust, and war; and how she thought that she would someday convince Gilgamesh to take her for his Queen. Shamhat was quite transparent to one as wise as Nininsina, and she would not have her Son, the Son of a Goddess no less, involved with a lowly concubine, much less marry her!

"How dare you enter my royal chamber without my permission!" Nininsina said to her, raising her voice. "Who do you think you are?!"

"Oh please Goddess," Shamhat replied, rather condescendingly. "It's not as though you could turn me into a donkey or something," she said giggling and wiggling her fingers in front of her. "Didn't you give up your power when you came down to Earth? Hmmm?"

Nininsina slowly approached Shamhat. Wavering for a moment in front of her, as Shamhat smirked mockingly at her, and with the speed of a leopard, she caught Shamhat by the throat and thrust her to the wall. As Shamhat gasped for breath, she tried in vain to pull Nininsina's hands from her neck, but the Goddess proved far too strong.

"I may have given up my place in the sky you little tramp," she began, "but I still have the power to snap your neck like a twig!" Shamhat continued to gasp for breath, as she could feel her vision blurring and the room beginning to spin. Just then, Gilgamesh walked through his mother's door.

"Mother!" he shouted at Nininsina. She looked back with a sadistic grin on her face. "Release her mother," Gilgamesh commanded. Nininsina released her grip and threw Shamhat to the floor beside her. Gilgamesh went over to where Shamhat had landed to see if she was all right. He rolled his eyes at Nininsina's behavior. His mother continued to grin, and chuckled as she walked away. It was not the first time that her temper had been taken out on one of his servants, Gilgamesh mused to himself; although she did seem to hate this one the most, he had noticed.

"What were you doing mother?" Gilgamesh inquired, almost amusedly. Nininsina simply smiled at her son and walked out of her chamber, stopping only to give Shamhat a little nudge with her foot on the way out. Shamhat was still trying to catch her breath. Glaring at Nininsina as she left the room, her attention turned toward Gilgamesh. Her eyes welled up in tears as she cried, "your mother was trying to kill me!" Gilgamesh helped her up from the floor and put his arm around her shoulder.

"It wouldn't be the first time she tried, would it?" he said with a grin. Shamhat was not amused, and she pulled her shoulder away from his arm. "Why must you repeatedly come here to fight with my mother each night Shamhat?" Shamhat didn't answer. She walked away from Gilgamesh, obviously hurt that he found it amusing that Nininsina was trying to harm her. But then again, what did she expect? After all, in the grand scheme of life, she was nothing more than a concubine, and Nininsina was a Goddess. She wasn't sure what compelled her to provoke her at every turn. It was always a serious character flaw that had her in trouble more than a few times in her life. In fact, it was this defiance that had caused her father to abandon her when she was a child. But perhaps she enjoyed taunting Nininsina because of how much she despised her. A bit of danger and overwhelming obstacles was what she had thrived on. She loved the challenge in a way. So much so that she was still convinced that she would have Gilgamesh in the end, despite Nininsina and the overwhelming odds. She was absolutely sure of it!

Shamhat turned back toward Gilgamesh and composed herself. Wryly she asked, "So, are you off to be with Siduri?" Gilgamesh nodded. Shamhat took a deep breath, still pouting, and hoping to curry some sympathy from him. Gilgamesh simply shook his head, and then turned and left the room for his chamber where Siduri was waiting for him. Dejectedly, Shamhat sat down on the foot of Nininsina's bed. She would get Nininsina back, she vowed to herself. Shamhat wasn't sure exactly how, but she *would* do it! And as for Siduri, Shamhat only hoped that she would do as she had advised her so Gilgamesh would be displeased and never call for her again!

---------------------------------------------------------------------------

Adad and Agga both waited patiently by the entrance to the forest. They had been returning there for several nights, hoping to catch a glimpse of whoever it was that was setting the animals free from their traps. They had been living on fish and fruits for some time now, and were starving for any other type of meat to kill the banality of their meals. It was still a mystery. Who would be so villainous as to steal another man's meal? Even the poorest of trappers and fishermen honored the code and each other's catch. If they could only find out who was responsible for the act, Adad thought. Gilgamesh had long since passed a law in the beginning of his reign that any man who was caught stealing from another would be executed in the most cruel way; not only that, but the person they had wronged would be the one to personally dole out the punishment. The King demanded absolute order among his subjects, and even the smallest of crimes were taken very seriously. This heavy-handedness was met with mixed reaction from his people, some loving it, some hating it, but it had kept everyone in fear for many years regardless. Adad was certainly no fan of Gilgamesh, but when it came to his livelihood, he agreed whole-heartedly with this law!

Agga stood up from where he and his father were sitting. They each had a long wooden pole right next to them, in case they met up with the criminal responsible.

"Father, did you hear that?" Agga asked, picking up his pole in his right hand. Adad listened for a moment, and then shook his head.

"What did you hear my son?" he asked Agga.

"It was something.....like the leaves rustling."

"It could simply be the wind," Adad responded.

"No father, it was the sound of someone walking, and the leaves crumpling beneath their feet," Agga reasoned. "I am sure of it!"

Adad squinted at the entrance to the forest where they had laid their trap. They had been fortunate enough to have had one trap that this criminal had not had a chance to free the animal from a few days before. In it they had caught a small rabbit, and ever since they had been caring for it at their home, all the while planning to use it as bait to lure whoever was doing this out in the open, and into entrapment! Now they had set the rabbit in the trap at the entrance to the forest, hoping to draw out the culprit.

"Shhh, quiet!" Adad whispered softly but firmly. Both he and Agga hid behind a large stone that was several hundred feet away from the rabbit and the entrance of the forest. They could hear something approaching, cautiously. Adad and Agga readied their poles. Then something became visible. It was strange looking. Almost like a bear; but a bear that was walking on two feet like a man. It was covered in shaggy hair from head to toe, but the walk was too light and graceful for a bear. Agga looked at his father with a confused look. Adad returned the favor. Then both of them turned their attention once again to the thing approaching; only in that short few seconds, it was gone.

"What happened to it?" Agga whispered. Adad shook his head in confusion.

"I don't know," he replied. "It was just there a second ago." Agga raised his head upward, as he heard a rustling above in the trees.

"Look father!" Agga exclaimed, pointing to the top of a tall tree at the entrance to the forest. They could see the branches swaying, just as they had several days ago when they first noticed the traps were being sprung.

"What the hell is it?!" Adad said, now becoming a little bit nervous. Maybe it hadn't been such a good idea to try to confront whatever was setting the animals free, Adad thought. He had assumed it was an ordinary thief of some kind, but clearly this was nothing ordinary. It walked like a man, but whatever it was, was clearly some kind of animal. Perhaps a breed that no one had ever seen before.

Both Adad and Agga fell backwards onto the ground, startled by the loud thud of something landing right next to their trap. Quickly they both crawled back behind the stone and peeked above the top of it to get a look at what it was. It *was* a man! At least it looked like one, and he was covered in fur like an animal. Adad's eyes scanned up and down as he realized this thing had jumped down from the top of the tree where the branches had been swaying. It had to have been a 40 or 50 foot drop! It was him they must have seen days ago, when the tree branches were swaying the same way without any wind at all. The strange man stood very tall, at least seven feet high!

Slowly the man-animal creature leaned over and began to let out the rabbit from the trap, all the while looking over at the rock, where Adad and Agga were both hiding in fear. After the trap door was opened, the rabbit ran away into the forest. The strange looking perpetrator then stood up straight and faced directly toward the rock, his eyes glowing in a brilliant fiery red color. Adad and Agga ducked their heads so as not to be seen, but it seemed that he sensed they were there anyway. He began to walk slowly toward the rock, almost stalking them. Agga and his father were both shaking as they held the poles close to their chest, both hoping they would not have to fight this strange creature. They could hear the footsteps coming closer. Then they suddenly stopped. Adad looked over at Agga. He had his eyes closed and was beginning to weep with fear. His heart pounding and his body still shaking, Adad poked his head up over the top of the rock to see where the strange thing was. He couldn't see it. It was if it had vanished!

"Get up boy," Adad told his son, still shaken. Agga shook his head and remained lying on the ground behind the rock with his eyes shut. "It's gone now Agga," Adad reassured him. He let out a few long breaths of relief, and scanned the area around the entrance of the forest for any sign of the creature. He didn't find any. Scratching his head in befuddlement, he pondered how the man thing could have disappeared so quickly. Did he run back into the forest? Impossible, he would have to run faster than a lion or deer to have done that. But then again, it seemed that anything was now possible. He had just witnessed a man covered in fur like an animal that had climbed to the top of a tree in a matter of seconds, and then jumped down without shattering his leg bones in a million pieces, as any normal man would have done.

He decided he must tell the King about this thing living in the forest. It was a threat to every trapper who trapped by the forest, and to every fisherman who fished on the beach directly adjacent to the forest. This man-animal had left them this time, but what about the next? A thing as strong and powerful as this could easily kill any man in a matter of seconds at his whim! Perhaps, he could even kill Gilgamesh Adad thought. He paused a moment as a grin came over his face. Kill Gilgamesh. Wouldn't that be wonderful, he mused, still smirking! Then Adad shook his head and came back to his senses. Despite the danger of returning to Uruk, which he had avoided doing for nearly 16 years, he felt he must warn the King so he could send out warriors to hunt this thing down. Not for himself, but for all the trappers and fishermen who were in danger from this thing. He knew he would not benefit from returning to Uruk; if anything, he was walking directly into danger!

"Get up," Adad ordered. Agga slowly stood up, all the while still grasping his pole tightly in his fists. "We must go to the palace in Uruk my son."

"Why must we go there father?" Agga asked, surprised his father would even suggest such a thing. From the time he could remember, Adad had taught him that Uruk was an evil place full of evil people. Now he wanted to go there?

"We must tell the King about this thing living in his forest. It could be deadly and kill many trappers and fishermen who come near here!"

Agga looked down at the sand for a moment, and then looked at his father. "But Uruk is a long way father. It will take us several days to travel there," Agga complained.

"Nevertheless, we must not think of just ourselves Agga," Adad replied sternly. Agga opened his mouth to complain again, but stopped as Adad glared at him. "Just do as I say! We will go home and pack some things for the trip tonight. I want to personally be the one that informs Gilgamesh about this thing," he told Agga.

"But we've never even been to Uruk," Agga said to him.

"I have my son," Adad told him. Agga stared at his father with a confused look. "I once lived there a long time ago; with your mother." Agga continued to stand there, bewildered by what his father said. As far as he knew, they had lived where they were all their lives. What did he mean that he had lived in Uruk many years ago with mother? Why didn't he ever tell him that? Adad turned away from Agga and stared out at the water for a moment.

"I'm an old man now. I have escaped destiny for many years, and it is time that I faced my demons," Adad said to himself aloud. Agga still stood and stared at his father, wondering what he was talking about. "Surely he won't even remember who I am now," Adad continued. "How could he? He must have encountered many people, every day since I left. Anyway, I have been fortunate enough to have eluded Gilgamesh for all these years; I can't hide myself or family forever in this remote, forsaken place."

Agga wasn't exactly sure what his father was rambling on about, but he knew better than to cross him. He guessed they would be making the long trip to Uruk, whether he liked it or not. What a burden! Personally, he would be happier simply eating fish and berries instead of making the excruciating journey all the way to Uruk. Even if they had horses it was a long way to the great city, but all they had were two broken down asses! What could be worse, Agga thought to himself?

-------------------------------------------------------------------------------

All of the girls in the harem were abuzz when Siduri had returned that night from Gilgamesh's chamber. She had actually been smiling, something which none of the concubines had ever done after a night with the King. Aruru had tried to question Siduri about the details, but all she had received were non-answers that never really satisfied her curiosity. But Shamhat had made her talk, and she was furious when she had found out that Siduri had apparently enjoyed her night with Gilgamesh. Never once had Gilgamesh acted as tender with her as he did with Siduri. Apparently, Gilgamesh had taken quite a liking to Siduri, more than any girl he had been with before. Not only was he gentle with her as they made love, but he had given her a gift of a pure gold necklace which was very valuable. He had requested that she come back the next night again.

After Shamhat was done interrogating Siduri, she had gone back to her own room to sulk and think about her own future. Perhaps it was time to give up her quest for

Gilgamesh, she thought to herself. She had been with him for years now and he had never given *her* a gift of any kind! He enjoyed making love to her, but he had never treated her, or any girl, that way he had Siduri; and it was killing Shamhat! As she sat on her bed and wept, Aruru knocked, and then entered her room.

"What's the matter," Aruru queried. Shamhat didn't even look up at Aruru as she shook her head and buried her head in her knees. She was embarrassed to be seen like this, having always played the role of a strong woman of authority in the harem. Aruru walked over and put her hand on her shoulder.

"It's because of Siduri, isn't it?" she guessed. Shamhat wiped the tears from her eyes and sighed deeply.

"Yes," she replied weakly. She got up from her bed and began pacing the floor as she spoke to Aruru. "For all the years I have been serving Gilgamesh.....and then to have him treat that little whore so well!"

"She's just a new toy," Aruru assured Shamhat. "After a while he will tire of her as he does every girl, send her away, and then ride into the city at the full moon to find a new girl. But he has always kept you around. That must mean something, right?"

Shamhat shrugged her shoulders. "Sometimes I'm not sure why he keeps me around. I'm not as beautiful as I once was," she stated matter-of-factly. "Or as young either."

"That's crazy," Aruru told her. "You are only 19 for goodness sakes!" Aruru put her hand on Shamhat's shoulder. "Listen, how about I whip up one of my special drinks for Siduri?" she said, grinning from ear to ear. Shamhat knew what she meant, and she couldn't help but crack a smile herself. Aruru was uneducated and not very refined, but had always had a talent for alchemy. It was an odd little hobby of hers, who knew why, but she had done it since she was a little girl. She knew that Aruru could make a drink that was sweet tasting, but deadly, in a variety of ways. Shamhat had called upon her to make some concoctions the last time she had felt threatened by a girl in the harem. When Gilgamesh had questioned them about where she had gone to, Shamhat had told him she snuck out and fled in the night. But with Siduri, she didn't think they could get away with it. While it was tempting, she knew that if Gilgamesh ever found out, he would probably execute the both of them! It was but by the luck of the Gods before that Gilgamesh had never suspected them of doing away with one of his concubines, and she didn't want to risk it again; especially since he seemed to care much more about this one than any other before.

"That's alright," Shamhat said to Aruru.

"I suppose it would be kind of strange to kill her anyway," Aruru said.

"Why do you say that?" Shamhat asked, a bit befuddled.

"Well, it's just that she looks so much like you," she replied. "Except for the eyes of course. It would be like

53

poisoning my best friend!" Shamhat stared at Aruru for a moment, wondering what she meant. She looked nothing like that tramp Siduri! Stupid Aruru! How could she even see any resemblance between her and that little whore of a girl?!

"So what are you going to do then?" Aruru inquired, breaking the silence.

"I don't know," said Shamhat. She paced the floor a few more times before saying, "I think maybe I should make a trip to Mari in the morning."

"Why Mari?" Aruru asked, puzzled.

"It is where the temple of Ishtar lies."

Aruru was confused. "Why would you want to go there?" she asked.

"I had a very strange dream a while ago," Shamhat told her. "It has been on my mind ever since. Maybe I can have the High Priestess of the temple interpret this dream for me. I am certain it was sent to me by Ishtar."

"How do you know that?" asked Aruru.

"I just know."

"Still," Aruru said, "do you think you should really leave right now? What about Siduri, shouldn't you be doing something to distract Gilgamesh from her?"

Shamhat put her hands up to the sides of her head. "I don't know!" she exclaimed, flopping down on her bed.

She felt as though her head would explode. What *should* she do? She felt as though the dream was a significant one; maybe it would even take her in a new direction of greatness, perhaps even to be the High Priestess one day! She had been pursuing Gilgamesh for years now, and seemed no closer to her goal than she did before. But then again, she longed desperately to one day be Queen. She lusted for power more than anything. What to do? A High Priestess had power over the servants of the temple, but no real glory. It was a life of servitude to Ishtar and not much else. And while Ishtar and her glorious stories fascinated her, she wanted *real* power. The kind she could only achieve by being Queen!

As she paced the floor trying to decide what to do, Shamhat and Aruru heard a commotion coming from the front gate to the palace. Her chambers were located very close to the entrance and she frequently was aware of anyone's comings and goings. There was an old man yelling and resisting as a guard was bringing him to a holding box, a type of solitary jail that sat near the entrance to the palace. There were a dozen of them, all made of cedar, and they were mainly used to imprison those subjects who had broken one of Gilgamesh's various frivolous laws. Some of them had been imprisoned for things such as stealing bread or dates. But some had been put there for things such as looking at another man's woman too long, or scratching themselves in public. There were many absurd laws that Gilgamesh made up on a whim either when he was in one of his fits of rage; or simply to amuse himself.

The old man struggled with the guards as they threw him into the holding box. It was only big enough for a man to stand or sit in and only had a tiny window big enough only to see in with one eye. Shamhat scurried out of her room down to the box, Aruru following right behind her.

"What do you suppose he did?" Aruru asked Shamhat.

"Only the Gods know," she replied. "You know how Gilgamesh is. It could be anything." Then she looked at Aruru. "I have to find out!"

"Why?" asked Aruru, raising an eyebrow. "What do you care about that old man for?"

"I don't know," Shamhat said, shaking her head. She looked out the window at the holding box again and stared at it. "There is just something familiar about him. I just don't know what it is." Aruru cocked the other eyebrow and looked at her as if she were nuts as Shamhat left her chambers and went out to the holding box. She peered into the box with her right eye. The old man was sitting with his knees to his chest, weeping. He had obviously been beaten as his eyes were both beginning to swell, and there was blood coming from his mouth.

"What is it you have done old man?" Shamhat asked of him. The old man didn't look at her. He just kept weeping like a child. "Come on old man, and tell me what you have done. Maybe I can help you." Actually Shamhat had no authority to help anyone other than her concubines, but she wanted him to talk. There was something about this man. It was as though she knew him before. She had never laid eyes on him until this day, but she felt as though they had some sort of connection.

The old man looked up at her slowly, tears still streaming from his eyes down his cheeks.

"What is your name?" Shamhat asked him.

"Adad," he replied meekly, after a moment.

"And why have the guards put you into this holding box?" She inquired. The old man put his hands up to his eyes and wiped away his tears.

"I came here with my son......to inform the King of a great danger," he said with a weak voice.

"What great danger Adad?" Shamhat asked him. He began to weep again.

"I shouldn't have come back," he muttered.

"Come on old man, tell me what you are talking about or I won't help you," Shamhat pressed.

Adad shook his head and began to speak, "There is something in the forest, near the Zagros Mountains where I live; something horrible!"

"What is so horrible?" Shamhat asked him. Adad sniffed as his nose was still oozing blood slowly, and then he took a deep breath and continued.

"I don't know. It was like an animal, but it walked like a man," he said quietly, shaking his head. "This thing had been springing our traps for many weeks, and when we tried to catch it....." He couldn't finish his sentence. Adad began to weep again.

"And where is your son?" Shamhat asked him. "You said you came here with your son." Adad began to cry harder. "What happened to your son Adad?"

"When we approached the gate to the city," Adad began with a stutter in his voice because of his tears, "we told the guards of what we saw in the forest. They didn't take us seriously. They began to laugh and taunt us. My son got angry and began to argue with one of the guards.....then they.....they.....they put an axe through his chest! The bastards!" he cried out, then put his head between his knees again. Shamhat had sympathy for this man. And she believed his story; at least she thought she did. It was an extraordinary story for sure, and many poor people had tried several ruses to try to get through the city gates before, but somehow she felt this man was different from the others.

"What was this thing you saw in the forest?" Shamhat asked Adad. Adad wiped the tears from his eyes again, and looked up at Shamhat.

"You believe me then?" he asked her in amazement.

"Yes, I do," she stated. Adad calmed down for a moment so he could explain after hearing that she believed him. He felt he could trust her, though he didn't know why.

"It was tall, about 10 feet high!" he exclaimed.

"Ten feet high?" Shamhat asked him with a half-believing look on her face.

"Yes, it was very tall and covered in hair like a bear or something.....and yet, it walked like you and me. Like any ordinary person!"

"Why was this thing springing your traps?" She asked.

"I don't know," he murmured. Shamhat stood for a moment in silence. She felt the need to help this man, but she could not risk being seen by the guards. Not even her favor with the King would save her from execution if she were caught releasing him. Adad continued to shake his head and talk to himself, almost inaudibly.

"I wish I could help you Adad," Shamhat said to him. He looked up at her and then nodded his head in acceptance of his fate.

"I know. I wouldn't want you to risk your life for someone you barely know anyway," he told her. Shamhat felt a tear fall from her eye. She genuinely felt sorry for this man who had just lost his son horrifically, and now faced death himself.

Shamhat turned to leave. "Those red eyes," Adad whispered to himself. "Those red eyes........"

"What did you say?" Shamhat asked Adad, stopping and turning back around slowly.

"I can't get them out of my head," he mumbled.

"Adad, tell me again what you just said!" she insisted.

"I just," he began, then paused to take a deep breath, "I just remember those eyes; the eyes of the beast!"

"What about them?"

"They were the strangest color. It was as if they glowed, you know, like a cat in the moonlight. But they were red!" Adad recalled, still chilled by the memory of them. Shamhat turned from Adad and her heart raced. It sounded familiar; the animal like man, the red glowing eyes. She knew the eyes he was describing. It sounded like the image of the beast she had seen in her vision from Ishtar! What did this mean? Could it be that this man was somehow connected to the vision she had? She wasn't sure, but she was compelled to find out more about this man-beast Adad had seen in the forest. She needed to find out why Ishtar had sent this vision to her, and why by chance she had met this stranger who had seen the same thing. At that moment, it didn't matter that she would be risking her life; she knew that she must free this man so he could take her to the forest.

-------------------------------------------------------------------------

Siduri sat cross legged on the floor of her father's home. After spending a few nights in a row with Gilgamesh he had released her for the night, and allowed her to go back to her father, Dagon. Gilgamesh had never done this before, and it wrought the ire of the other concubines. Dagon was astonished at this act, but eternally grateful that his daughter was back safe and sound. He had expected to never see his daughter again until she turned 18, and even then, who knew what to expect after all the savage treatment! It had completely broken character for the King to release any concubine before she had reached 18 years of age, nor to allow any of them to leave the palace grounds at any time during their tenure with him.

"I still don't understand how, but I am thankful," Dagon said to Siduri. She smiled and continued to pour water into the flour bowl to make dough for bread. Dagon got up from where he was sitting and went outside to buy some wine to go with dinner. He gave Siduri a kiss on her head on the way out. Since her mother had died a few years before, she had taken the lead woman's role in the household for her father, cooking and cleaning, and taking care of her father. Her mother had died from some disease, though the Asu, or doctor, had been unable to figure out why she was dying. It had been a tragic time, but they had managed to get through it. Siduri felt bad for her father; a few years before to lose his wife, and then to lose her to Gilgamesh. She felt terrible!

As she was kneading the dough, a neighbor woman came popping in the doorway. She and her husband ran a small spice shop in the town and had known their family for years.

"Oh my god," she exclaimed, and ran over to give Siduri a hug. "My husband told me that you had been released and were home, but I thought he was nuts! The King never releases girls that soon!"

"I guess I'm just special Antum," Siduri said to the woman with an embarrassed smile on her face. "Anyway, how did he know about it?"

"Your father, of course," she told her. "You know they still go out and fish at the Euphrates together from time to time." Antum walked about the room whistling to herself. Siduri could tell she wanted something, but she kept kneading her dough and keeping her mouth shut.

"So tell me dear girl," Antum said, coming over and standing right behind Siduri, "What about the King?"

"What?" Siduri replied. Antum leaned close to her ear.

"What was it like to be with him?" Antum inquired in a whisper, in case Dagon was anywhere nearby. Siduri blushed and smiled. "Come on now child, I have to know." Siduri wasn't sure if she should talk about it. Antum was known as being quite the gossiper of the city, and the last thing they needed was for word to get back to the palace that she had been giving details about their night together.

"It was nice," was all she offered to Antum.

"Just nice? That's it?"

"Yes. He was very kind with me."

Antum raised an eyebrow in disbelief. "I've heard from many girls that he is quite the harsh lover," she stated. Siduri shook her head.

"I heard the same stories from the other girls in the harem," she began, "but he was very gentle with me when we made love. And it didn't happen right away because we spent a lot of time talking first."

"Talking?!" Antum almost shouted in disbelief. Siduri nodded and continued to knead the dough. "The King.....Gilgamesh the Great.....He talked to you? Like we're talking now?"

"Yes."

"I've always talked to many of the people from the palace when they visit my shop for supplies, and none of them ever have had a conversation with the King! The only person he talks to is his wretched mother; and his military generals of course," Antum stated, still in disbelief. "And you say that you talked with him before he had his way with you?"

"Yes we did; for a long time too," Siduri told Antum, beginning to get a little irritated with the whole conversation. She wanted to tell Antum to just go away and mind her own business, but she was too shy to do that. Still, Antum was pushing Siduri's patience. "I actually learned a lot about him, and he's not that bad a person."

"Are you crazy child?" Antum asked her. "Have you seen his behavior in this Kingdom? Didn't he just barge in here one night and take you without your consent or that of your father?" Siduri just kept kneading her dough. "And doesn't he execute people for something as small as stealing bread? Even the Assyrians, those uncivilized animals, don't kill each other for this! And you say he's not that bad a person?!"

Siduri's patience had run out. She stopped kneading and set the bowl aside. Standing up, she looked right into Antum's eyes.

"I am tired of this conversation now Antum. Could you just please leave now?!" Siduri said with a serious expression on her face. Antum was a little taken aback. She had never seen Siduri speak so directly to her or any elder person. They stood and stared at each other for a moment, neither one knowing just what to say. It was an awkward moment. Just then Dagon walked through the door of his home and found the two women staring at each other as if they were about to begin a duel to the death.

"What's going on here ladies?" he cautiously asked. Antum said nothing. She turned and walked past Dagon, nearly bumping into him, and out the door quickly. Siduri sighed with relief as the tension had finally been broken by her father. She took the dough out of the clay bowl and began to pound it into shape.

"What was that all about?" Dagon asked, putting his arm around his daughter's shoulder.

"Nothing father," she said quietly, shaking her head.

"Come on, tell me what happened," Dagon insisted.

"She was just asking me about what happened with Gilgamesh that night we spent together."

"Hmm, that's a little personal of a question," Dagon exclaimed, chuckling. Siduri nodded. "That old busybody should mind her own business sometimes!"

"It is okay father," Siduri assured him.

"So that's why you were mad at her?"

"It wasn't just that," Siduri said, pounding the dough as they talked. "We were arguing because I told her that he wasn't such a bad person as everyone thinks."

Dagon cocked his head and looked at her. "Why do you say that?" he asked her, his mood changing. Siduri stopped working on the dough and looked at her father.

"Not you too?" she pleaded.

"You have to admit that he's done terrible things during his reign," Dagon pointed out to her, sitting down on the floor. "Not the least of which was kidnapping you for his harem!"

"I know he has father," she answered. She felt the tears coming to her eyes. Siduri turned to her father and asked, "Have you ever known me to lie to you father?"

"Of course not," he said to her, standing up and holding her as she began to weep. He rocked her back and forth as he held her. It was something he used to do when she was little to calm her down when she cried. "Well, maybe you saw a side of him that we never get to see I guess." Siduri nodded, her head still buried in his chest. Dagon didn't really mean it, but he wanted to comfort his daughter. In his heart, he hated Gilgamesh, and always would!

"He talked to me about everything. His mother, the Kingdom, his concerns......even his fears," she said, sniffing as her nose was runny. Dagon listened in amazement. Never before had he heard anyone describe Gilgamesh in any humanistic way.

"So he really talked to you, I mean, about things?" Dagon asked. Siduri nodded her head.

"I felt sorry for him in a way," she said.

"Sorry for him? Why?" Dagon asked.

"He feels real pain sometimes that the people in his Kingdom hate him to such a degree." Siduri said. She turned to her father. "Do you know what else he told me?" Dagon shook his head. "He told me that he and his mother had some sort of strange dream about a man. And that this man would threaten him as King, and that this man was coming soon." Siduri turned away and continued. "He seemed, almost.....scared. Can you imagine? Gilgamesh, the mighty Gilgamesh afraid of anything?"

"No, I can't even imagine," Dagon replied truthfully.

"But he was father, and for that one moment, he wasn't this all powerful ruler of Sumeria. He wasn't the cruel King of Uruk who killed men at his whim or kidnapped young women to be his concubines. For that one moment he was just like any other man. And I felt pity for him." Siduri looked at her father, and he begrudgingly nodded his head in understanding.

"I must return tomorrow night to the palace; for dinner with Gilgamesh," Siduri told her father. Dagon looked at her for a moment, not knowing how to respond to it. "And.....I *want* to go father."

Dagon sighed and shrugged his shoulders. He managed to squeeze out and "okay" to her as he saw he would not change her mind. Siduri smiled.

"Thank you father," she happily chirped.

He got up from where he was sitting and gave Siduri a hug before he strolled out the door of his home again. Siduri went back to preparing dinner for her father. She was chopping garlic, leeks, and onions which would be made into stew. She felt a huge weight off her chest, and she gleefully hummed as she cooked. After cooking the vegetables, she would add a little bit of Cumin spice, just like her father liked it, and then cook them all into the bread she had made to make a pie. Her father always loved that. Sometimes she would even make the pie with mutton or some other meat, but tonight she was keeping it simple. She was exhausted from her past few days experience in the palace after all.

Outside the sun was setting in the distance, and Dagon went out to the stable next to the house, where he kept his horse. He often went there in the evenings before dinner. It was relaxing to spend some time grooming his horse, usually while he thought about what types of modifications he could make to his weapons he made and sold to the royal army. His socket axe had been hugely successful in battle, and had earned Gilgamesh's army superiority over any other army; as if having a King who was part God wasn't enough of an advantage!

Tonight, though, he was thinking only of his daughter, and what she had just told him about Gilgamesh. Dagon had always hated him since the death of his wife and he had always blamed him for the event. There were so many things that Siduri just didn't understand about what he had done to their family; so many things he hadn't told her about her *real* mother. If she knew, she probably wouldn't be so keen to have dinner with him, or get so close, he thought! His daughter was very intelligent though, and she could always see into a person's heart and soul. Whenever she met someone for the first time, she could tell right off if that person was bad or good. And for whatever reason, she had looked into the heart of Gilgamesh and found some goodness. And it seemed she wanted to spend some time with him. Dagon would just have to accept that for now, like it or not!

-------------------------------------------------------------------------

"How much farther is it old man?" Shamhat asked Adad.

"Not much farther," he assured her. It seemed they had been riding forever. How long did it take to reach the great forest anyway? They were riding two horses she had taken from the royal stable, horses in fine physical condition, usually used by Gilgamesh's army during battles. If it took this long on the horses, she wondered how long had it taken Adad and his son to make it to Uruk on those broken down asses they had ridden!

"I'm getting tired and hungry," Shamhat complained.

"We can stop at my home if you wish," Adad told her.

"Forget it," she said. His home had to be that of a very simple man, and she was royalty. Well, sort of royalty, being the head concubine, but certainly after she had been living in the palace for so long, she couldn't humble herself to stay even a moment in a poor man's house. It would be beneath her!

Just then, Adad turned to her and pointed to the distance. There she could see the outline of several mighty trees in the horizon. Finally they had the entrance to the forest in their sights. Her heart began to pump very quickly, and her breaths came shorter as they drew closer. She knew she believed that Ishtar had directed her to be there, and it had something to do with this beast Adad had seen, but beyond that, she didn't know exactly what to expect. It was all a little bit frightening now. The image of the beast she had visions of in her dreams were as terrifying as they were exciting. The reality of what she was doing was beginning to set in, and she was beginning to question whether or not it was a good idea to be there after all. What if this thing tore her to pieces? And what was she supposed to do when she met it anyway? In her dream she lay down with the beast and it made wild love to her, and in the dream it was all very surreal. But this wasn't a dream anymore. This was reality, and the reality of meeting this thing in the forest could be very different!

As she struggled with what to do in her mind, she hadn't noticed that the entrance to the forest was almost on top of them now. It couldn't have been but several hundred feet away now. The trees of the forest were ominous to say the least. They were taller than any tree she had ever seen before, and they were all clustered together and as thick as carpet. You couldn't see into the forest from the outside. She wondered if the inhabitants of the forest had ever seen the sun before. It looked impossible for the rays to even penetrate the thickness of the trees everywhere. Adad looked back at Shamhat.

"Are you sure you want to do this?" he asked. Shamhat stopped her horse dead in its tracks and stared at the forest entrance. She took a deep breath as she pondered her next move. "Well, are you going to go in or not?" Adad asked Shamhat. She still didn't move or say a word. There were a torrent of thoughts and emotions running through her as she sat frozen on her horse.

"I don't think I can do this," she said in an almost inaudible voice. Adad leaned closer to her, trying to discern what she was saying. Just then, he could hear the swaying of the trees. It was an all too familiar sound to him now. His heart began to race. He got off his horse and looked quickly from side to side.

"What is it?" Shamhat nervously asked, dismounting her horse as well. Adad put his finger to his lips and motioned for her to be quiet.

"It's here," he whispered. Shamhat could feel her stomach turn and her breaths quicken in fright. Adad kept scanning the area near the forest entrance for any sign of the creature he had encountered before.

"Where is it?" Shamhat worriedly asked. Now she was really beginning to doubt the logic behind this journey. How could she trust a vision from Ishtar anyway? She was the most mischievous of all the Gods or Goddesses. It was foolish of her to follow a dream that may or may not have been from the Goddess. She was setting herself up to be slaughtered by some unknown thing roaming in the forest, and for what, she thought?

Adad's head turned as he heard the snapping of twigs and branches. He still couldn't see anything, but he knew that the thing he had encountered before was there, watching them. At any moment this thing could leap from the top of one of the trees outlining the entrance and pounce on them both. He had seen it jump down before!

"Let's get out of here!" Adad said nervously to Shamhat. "I don't know why you wanted to come here in the first place. I told you this thing could rip you apart in a second! Let's just go!" Adad mounted his horse and motioned for Shamhat to do the same. Shamhat was scared out of her wits, but she couldn't move. Something was compelling her to stand there, and before she could even fashion a rational thought, she found herself walking toward the entrance of the forest.

"What in the name of the Gods are you doing?!" Adad shouted out at her. It didn't faze her. She didn't even glance back his direction. She just kept slowly moving toward the entrance of the forest. As she got closer, she could hear sounds coming from the top of the trees in front of her. Looking up, she saw the branches swaying back and forth, but there was no wind. It looked as if something had been standing on a large branch near the top of the tree, and then leapt off. Shamhat's heart was pumping so hard she felt as if her chest would explode. Adad sat upon his horse and watched as if he were witnessing a tragic accident happening in front of his eyes; one that he couldn't stop. He wanted to leave, but it seemed that something was compelling him to stay also. He felt a connection to the girl; he didn't know why, but he wanted, no needed, to make sure she was safe.

Shamhat arrived at the entrance to the forest. It was eerily dark and silent. She could only see a few feet in front of her as the trees and bushes were abnormally thick. Her eyes darted back and forth, looking for any signs of life. There were none. It was all so odd. She expected that a forest would be brimming with life; birds, rabbits, or something. There was complete silence. The tree tops were no longer swaying as they had been before. It was unnerving actually. Shamhat took a deep breath, and then slowly took a few steps forward; still nothing. Looking back at Adad, who was still sitting at a distance on his horse and watching, she threw up her hands at finding nothing more than disturbing silence in the forest. Adad shrugged his shoulders back at her. He was certain there was something there. There had to be. He couldn't have imagined it! What he and his son had seen was real, he was sure of that.

"There's nothing here you crazy old man!" Shamhat yelled to Adad. She was fuming that he had brought her all the way out to the forest with his wild tales of man-beasts. Maybe the dream she had was not from Ishtar after all. She wondered how she could be so foolish as to listen to this old lunatic!

"There *is* something there. I swear it!" Adad shouted back to her. Shamhat began to walk away from the forest entrance when her eyes became wide and she froze in her tracks. She felt something pulling at her hair from behind her. Adad thought he saw something stir behind Shamhat and he squinted his eyes to try and make out what it was. And then she was gone. In an instant he saw her disappear from sight. The entrance to the forest was dark and quiet once again as Shamhat had vanished in the blink of an eye!

Adad didn't know what to do. He couldn't return and tell Gilgamesh that Shamhat had disappeared in the forest. Surely he would be imprisoned again. For that matter, he would probably be executed for leading her there! It was only luck that he had escaped the wrath of Gilgamesh all those years ago and more recently a few days ago; now it would be suicide to ever return to Uruk again!

"I should have never gone back," he whispered to himself, still staring into the forest entrance, wrought with guilt. Now he was responsible for the deaths of two people, he told himself. He could only imagine what fate would befall Shamhat now. He prayed that somehow she was all right, even if it was a seeming pipe dream now. Adad turned his horse away from the forest and slowly headed for his home. He stopped for a moment and peered back at the entrance. There was still nothing. He wasn't sure what he would do now. He wanted to help her, but there would be nothing he could physically do against whatever it was he had seen before at his age.

Adad kicked his horse's side and headed for his home. His home was empty, his son and wife gone now. It seemed the only thing left for him now would be to wait for death to come.  It seemed to be the only comforting thought left to him now. It was probably what he deserved though, he thought. He was now personally responsible for the deaths of two people, he kept telling himself; not to mention his wife and family years before. Adad was riddled with guilt. The Sumerians believed that people ravaged with illness and bad luck were products of their own sin. He wasn't sure, but perhaps his sins from his past were coming to plague him now. First, by the death of Agga, and now Shamhat, not to mention his failing health, which had begun to burden him just after he had encountered that strange beast of the forest.

Adad turned to look back at the forest entrance one last time before it became a blur on the horizon. It was such a waste, he thought. Shamhat was something special, he could tell when he met her and she had taken the time to listen. She was beautiful, beguiling, and savvy; a character like no other. Over the past few days they had traveled together, he had grown quite fond of her, despite her constant complaining and snobbish attitude. Gilgamesh would be enraged to lose her.  Surely there was no one quite like her in his entire Kingdom. He always wished he had a daughter like her; but then again, long ago, he did. Adad shook his head and began to weep. It was such a foolish waste!

------------------------------------------------------------------------

Siduri lay quietly in the bed and looked around the room at all of the exotic things in Gilgamesh's chamber. She hadn't really noticed them the first time she was there. There was too much going on in her mind at the time. But now that she felt at ease being there again, she couldn't help but marvel at Gilgamesh's marvelous taste. She had been told by one of his servants that the King had decorated the room himself, an odd thing for a ruler to do. Usually there were others around the King who took care of such details, leaving the King to rule at all hours of the day. But Gilgamesh was different. He had a penchant for detail in everything he did, and always wanted to be involved. It was one of the reasons he was so successful in every endeavor; from combat, to legalities, and to even designing the palace he now resided in when he first made Uruk his central city from which to reign. Gilgamesh had been prepared all of his life by his mother to be ruler of all Sumeria, and when King Dumuzi's power had begun to fade, Gilgamesh was there, waiting to conquer him and take over the reins. He designed and helped build the great wall that encircled the city of Uruk, making an impenetrable barrier surrounding the city. Gilgamesh had handpicked every soldier in his army, ensuring that they were the most talented, loyal, and strongest fighters. He took great care to be part of every decision in his Kingdom, breaking the mold of past rulers.

Siduri heard the chamber door open. Gilgamesh walked in and saw Siduri waiting for him on his bed and smiled at her. He was very pleased that she had willfully accepted the offer to return, half expecting her not to come. He would have hated to have to come to Dagon's house and take her by force again. It was the first occasion since he became ruler that he had asked a woman to come to him. In the past he had simply ordered them. It was a bit messy at times, and Gilgamesh had to slaughter many fathers who tried to object in the beginning. Also, in the past, often the girls were very much unprepared to please him, causing him to be quite brutal with them. But this problem had been solved for many years after he had found Shamhat to keep order in his harem.

"I've been waiting for you my King," Siduri said, gazing seductively into Gilgamesh's eyes. He was absolutely intoxicated by her every time she spoke to him; and he had misjudged her as well. He had expected that she would be very shy and timid, but she was just the opposite in the bedroom. Yet at the same time, she had a purity and honesty that had led him to intrinsically trust her. He never had felt that same closeness with any of the other women, even Shamhat. Siduri was different. She was just as alluring as Shamhat, but also a woman of high integrity. Maybe even the perfect woman to be by a King's side, he mused.

"I didn't expect you to come," Gilgamesh said to Siduri. She slid off the bed and walked over to where he was standing. Putting her arms around his shoulders, she kissed him gently on the lips and neck. Gilgamesh let out a sigh of approval.

"I really felt like we connected last night," Siduri cooed at Gilgamesh. "I find you to be the most fascinating man I've ever met. I couldn't stay away from you."

"I don't know why you find me so fascinating," Gilgamesh told her. Siduri raised an eyebrow and giggled.

"You don't know why?" she asked. Gilgamesh shook his head. Siduri kissed him again, and then gazed into his eyes.

"I don't know why, but I feel like I can trust you," Gilgamesh told Siduri. This made Siduri quite happy to hear and she grinned from ear to ear. Gilgamesh sat down on his bed and Siduri sat down beside him. He had a concerned look on his face.

"What is the matter my King," Siduri asked him, rubbing her hands up and down his chest. Gilgamesh looked at her and shook his head.

"It's nothing," he replied.

"Come on and tell me," she said, now rubbing his back.

"It's just.........I haven't seen Shamhat for two days now," he told her.

"And this bothers you?" Siduri said rather cynically.

"Of course it does. She keeps order with all my servants and concubines," he replied. Siduri frowned disapprovingly.

"You know," Siduri began, "she isn't indispensible."

"She is to me!" Gilgamesh snapped back. He got up from the bed and paced the floor. "Why is it that everyone has something against Shamhat?"

"Maybe it's because of who she is," Siduri answered, rising from the bed also. "She is quite a manipulator. Everyone can see it. I have only been in the harem for a very short time, but I saw how she played games with everyone's mind; and how cruel she could be with all of the girls, and servants for that matter." Gilgamesh turned to face her and Siduri came close to him, looking him right in the eyes. "You only see the benefit of her service because she one day hopes to be your Queen. But all of your subjects who deal with her day in and day out have to take the brunt of her mistreatment and manipulative ways!" Siduri began to cry as she spoke. She really cared for Gilgamesh a great deal and wanted to make him see how Shamhat was plotting to be the most powerful woman in all of Sumeria by using him.

Gilgamesh grabbed Siduri's arms. He had never allowed anyone to talk back to him, except his mother of course; yet this girl dared to speak to him that forcefully, even though he barely knew her! Siduri turned her face to one side when he grabbed her and closed her eyes. Gilgamesh stared at her and then released his grip.

"What are you doing?" he asked her.

"I thought you were going to strike me for my lack of reverence my King," she told him in a dramatic fashion. Gilgamesh smiled, and then began to laugh. Just the way she had said it. She so amused him.

"You are laughing at me?" she asked.

"I can't help but adore you Siduri," he said to her.

"Yes, I do have a wicked sense of humor," Siduri told him, smiling playfully. "But I can be very serious too. You told me that you trust me; then trust me now when I tell you that Shamhat *cannot* be trusted! Her only thirst is for control and her only hunger is for power! She will try and trick you into making her your Queen so she can gain power, and then who knows? Maybe she will poison your wine, or give away secrets to the Assyrians and Egyptians. Believe me my King; she will bring destruction to your house!"

Gilgamesh sat and listened all the while that Siduri was speaking. In his head, he knew that it was true. His mother had echoed the same words before. Besides that, he was no fool; he was part Deity after all, and he was infused with the wisdom and strength of the Gods. But there was just something about Shamhat. Maybe it was because he had found her when his Kingdom was in a bit of disarray right after he had taken power and beaten back the Egyptians and Assyrians. Shamhat was manipulative and power hungry, he knew, but she was also a masterful politician, keeping his palace in order and his close servants happy. It was for this reason that he was so reluctant to just cast her aside for Siduri. On the other hand, he had kept Shamhat very close to him because he didn't entirely trust her either. But with Siduri, he knew that he could trust her to be, perhaps, his greatest confidant; besides his mother, of course.

"Perhaps it *is* time for a change," Gilgamesh said, pacing the floor of his bedroom once again. Siduri sat down at the foot of the bed and watched him. He kept pacing the floor for several minutes, then stopped and looked down at Siduri. She looked back at him in expectation.

"Since Shamhat has decided to simply leave without my consent or knowing, you will be in charge of the Harem and servants of the palace now." He told Siduri. It was the most pleasing thing she had ever heard in her life. She would be living in the palace with Gilgamesh and be a woman of great importance! Her father would be shocked and disappointed, of course, but she didn't care. This moment was the most satisfying of her life. She knew that fate and the Gods had drawn Gilgamesh to her, and she could be part of bringing compassion and sanity to his rule. It was as though it was meant to be, and that perhaps, on an unconscious level, she had always known.

Siduri leapt up at the news and showered Gilgamesh with kisses of gratitude. He returned the sentiment, and they were soon in a passionate lovelock. She pulled him down to the bed, and they enjoyed the rest of the night together.

Yes, it was meant to be, she was sure of it! But, she had to admit, she was curious herself. What did happen to Shamhat? And what would she do when she returned and found her place taken? Siduri didn't really care at the moment; she just knew that he had chosen the better woman in the end.

--------------------------------------------------------------------

Darkness; there was nothing but darkness when she opened her eyes. She could feel a gentle breeze blow by her and the rustling of leaves on the ground, yet she could not tell where she was. Something was moving; at least, it sounded as though something was. It was hard to say. She was barely conscious of anything. It felt as though she had awakened from a long slumber, and her cognitive abilities were still a bit hazy.

Shamhat tried to get to her feet, but she fell to the ground before she could gain her balance. She felt dizzy and nauseous. The trees surrounding her gave off a pungent smell. It was clear she was in the forest, but how did she get there? The last thing she remembered was standing at the entrance, yelling at Adad, that crazy old man that had brought her there in the first place. But then again, maybe he wasn't so crazy after all! Something had taken her deep inside the forest, but whom? Or what?

Her head was aching. She put the palm of her hand on top of her head and winced in pain. There was a knot that seemed the size of her fist there. That was why she was so groggy, she now realized. Something or someone had struck her and knocked her out, then brought her here. Inside the forest there was barely a hint of light that shined through the thickness of all the surrounding trees. There was a gentle breeze, but she suspected that there was never much more than this because the forest walls blocked most of the surrounding wind.

She was lucky to be alive, she thought to herself. For that matter though, *why* was she alive? Surely it could not have been a man who attacked her. What man could survive and live in this forest after all? But if it was an animal of some kind, why did it not kill her? It was all very odd and Shamhat didn't like it one bit. So many different thoughts were running through her mind at this moment. She was beginning to regret doubting the authenticity of the dream she had. Maybe she wasn't so foolish after all. Maybe it had been from the Goddess and there was some sort of beast living here. Perhaps it was fate that she had wound up in this situation. Why else was she alive now? There had to be a reason, Shamhat said to herself.

Shamhat's pulse raced and her breaths became short as she suddenly had the strangest sensation that she was being watched. Her eyes darted across the forest floor, but found nothing. Then again, it was hard to see anything at all in the darkness. She could hear the rustling of leaves on the trees behind her. She spun around quickly, trying to catch a glimpse of what it might be. There was nothing; only the swaying of branches in a nearby tree. Then she heard another noise to her right. She turned her head quickly and looked, but again, there was nothing more than the swaying of branches.  It seemed that the tree branches were being disturbed in a circular pattern around her. Something must be circling her, she thought to herself. Shamhat had had enough.

"Come out and show yourself!" she screamed as loud as she could. There was no reply. Her blood began to boil. She was becoming agitated and angry now. If this thing intended to kill her, she preferred it get on with it, instead of toying with her!

"I said come out and show yourself you cowardly beast!" she shouted again. There was nothing. It seemed that whatever was stalking her had ceased for the moment.

Suddenly, there was no movement at all. It was dead silent, and Shamhat became uneasy again. She decided to start walking. She didn't know where the entrance to the forest was anymore, but she thought she should try to find it. Slowly Shamhat began to walk in no particular direction. She wasn't sure where she was going, but anything was better than waiting to be slaughtered like cattle! Some branches cracked behind her, as if someone was following her. Shamhat began to walk faster, but whatever it was, was clearly following her every move. Shaking and completely frightened now, she began to run as fast as she could. There was nothing in front of her but forest and more forest, with no indication of where she was or how far the entrance might be. She continued to run, darting between trees and bushes, trying to elude whatever was following her. Finally, when she had run out of breath completely, she stopped. Gasping for air, she put her hand on the trunk of a tree and leaned against it. She looked back and to each side, but there was no sign of life. Perhaps she had finally escaped whatever it was. Shamhat still had no idea where she was though. All the trees looked alike and she still had no bearing as to where in the forest she might be. She put her hands on her knees and breathed deeply, trying to regain her breath and poise.

A roar was all she heard as she was thrown to the ground. Something had come out of nowhere and pushed her down. She let out a scream of terror as she finally got her first glimpse of what was following her. Standing before her was an incredibly tall figure. The shape was human, but it was covered in hair like a gorilla. It had red eyes that seemed to glow in the darkness; just like her dream, but this time, her fear didn't turn to excitement as this thing came closer to her! She wanted to get up and run, but she couldn't move. It seemed her legs had become like iron and weighed a thousand pounds. The figure moved closer to her and she closed her eyes and braced herself for an attack. Then it stopped, dead in its tracks. It cocked its head to one side and stared at her. Shamhat cracked one eye open to see what was happening, and was met by the most piercing eyes staring at her. She opened the other eye, and the figure cocked its head to the other side. It seemed to be examining her, like it had never seen a person before. In fact, it now almost seemed to be timid as it inquisitively stared at her.

Shamhat finally mustered the courage to stand up again. The beast towered over her, but still did not move; just carefully watched her from several feet away. Still trembling from the experience, Shamhat backed up a few steps. The towering figure moved a few steps forward. She backed up a few more, and the beast followed, always keeping a few feet distance between them.

"What do you want?" Shamhat asked the creature in a meek voice. It didn't answer her, but just continued to stare. "Please....." she stammered, "let me go." The beast did nothing. Shamhat began to feel tears roll down her cheeks as she felt she may not make it out of the forest alive. "Please let me go, I beg you," she wept. The beast didn't acknowledge, but seemed quite curious about the strange things coming from Shamhat's eyes. It started to move closer to Shamhat. She stepped back, but the beast came close to her before she could blink an eye. The quickness of his movement startled her, and she fell to the ground. The beast stood over her and extended his hand to her face.

"Why don't you just kill me then?!" Shamhat screamed, becoming hysterical. "Don't toy with me you bastard! Come on and kill me if you are going to kill me! Do it now!" Shamhat picked up a branch and threw it at the beast's head. It did little to distract it. Its hand continued to reach for her face until its finger was on her cheek. Trembling, Shamhat closed her eyes and waited for an attack. The beast took a teardrop from her cheek on its finger, then pulled its finger back and looked at it. Shamhat, tears streaming, opened her eyes and looked at the thing towering over her. She suddenly got the sense that it wasn't going to kill her after all. Wiping the tears from her eyes with her forearm, Shamhat stood up and faced the beast in front of her. She stared closely at its face. It almost seemed human the more she looked at it. Looking beneath the exterior of all the fur-like hair on its face, she could see the outline of what was underneath. The form was just like any normal man's face. It was astonishing!

Slowly, Shamhat's trembling and crying began to waiver, and her state of terror diminished. The beast had sat down near a tree close to the both of them, and was staring at its finger which had taken the tear from her eye. Suddenly her feeling about this thing that had taken her into the forest began to change. Strangely, she wasn't afraid of it anymore. The more she watched it closely, the

87

more human it began to look. His hair was thick all over his body, but he was still clearly a man. But how did a man come to live in the forest like an animal, she wondered? Had he been abandoned by his parents? Or were his parents killed and he left to grow up in the harshest of surroundings here in the forest? It was a mystery. And a mystery the Shamhat was suddenly very interested to solve. Something had compelled her to come here and make this discovery, and she was determined to find out who this man was and why she had dreamt of him. There had to be a higher purpose behind it.

Suddenly, the man stood up and scanned the area around them. Shamhat also looked from side to side to try and see what he was trying to find. Without a word, he crouched down, and then leapt to the top of a nearby tree.

"By the Gods!" Shamhat exclaimed, looking up at the top of the tree. She couldn't believe what she had just seen. He had to have jumped 30 feet straight up in the air! How was this possible? No man could do this. Not even Gilgamesh, whom she had once seen leap over a 7 foot wall and carry a nearly 1000 pound stone by himself on his shoulder, could do what she had just witnessed!

At the top of the tree, the strange man began to look out to the distance. Then, he leapt from one tree to the next, as graceful as anything Shamhat had ever seen. He stopped for a moment after leaping from one tree to another, then dropped down to the ground, several feet from where Shamhat stood. She heard a loud squeal of pain, and he seemed to be doing something vigorously with his hands, but his back was to her, and she couldn't quite make out what it was. After a moment, the man returned to Shamhat, carrying something. Shamhat squinted as he came close, trying to make out what he was carrying; and then she saw it. There was blood covering his hands and the limp body of a small white bird. He offered it to her, but Shamhat was still in shock. The blood was dripping from the fresh corpse as he held it out with his hands for her to take. Shamhat was disgusted. She turned her shoulder to him, but her apprehension to take the gift, she could see, was visibly upsetting her host. Closing her eyes, she held out her hands, and he placed the carcass in them, smiling in approval. Then he leapt to the top of another tree, and disappeared into the distance. Shamhat slowly opened her eyes and dropped the bird onto the ground in front of her. Grimacing in disgust, she kicked the bird's lifeless body away from her into a bush. She hoped that he would think she ate it and be pleased enough not to hurt, or even kill her.

"What now?" she whispered to herself, pacing back and forth. She didn't have any idea what to do. On one hand she sympathized with this man. God knows how he came to be in the forest and living like an animal, or how he could leap so high and do the extraordinary things he did. But she still felt she had been led there by more than chance. Perhaps even to help him. On the other hand though, she still had a little bit of trepidation about her whole situation. This man was untamed and wild. It could prove dangerous. I mean, what did she think she was going to do with this man anyway; rehabilitate him and bring him home for dinner?!

--------------------------------------------------------------------------

Gilgamesh knocked on the door to his mother's chamber. He received no reply. Turning to Shullat who was standing by his side, he shrugged his shoulders.

"What is she doing in there Lord?" Shullat asked Gilgamesh. "I mean, she has been in there for days now!"

"I don't know old friend," Gilgamesh told him. Nininsina had never sequestered herself away from Gilgamesh for such a long period of time before. She had always had a close eye on him and had a hand in every major decision he had. But as of late, she had been distant, especially since the disappearance of Shamhat. Gilgamesh would have thought that she would be very pleased that she had seemed to vanish without a trace. She never really did trust Shamhat. Since she had been gone though, Nininsina had locked herself in her chamber and refused to come out. She let in a servant at night to bring her food and water, but no one else. Not even her own son could bring her out of her room. It was all very odd.

"Do you think she's gone mad?" Shullat asked him. Gilgamesh gave him a look, and Shullat instantly changed the subject. "Perhaps she's ill. What if that's it Lord?"

"No," Gilgamesh began, before taking a deep breath.

"What is it then? I've never seen your mother this way."

"I don't know. The servant who brings her food each night has told me that she is always sitting and meditating."

"Meditating?" Shullat said.

"It's something she has always done, ever since I was a child," Gilgamesh told him. "She can see things.....visions and such." Shullat looked puzzled. He was a simple man and not too keen on many things but fighting and more fighting.

"What kind of visions?" Shullat inquired.

"All kinds," Gilgamesh responded. "They've been very useful over the years in foreseeing what my enemies might be doing, or what kind of decisions I must make to keep the Kingdom strong. She can see things from the Gods. Like dreams, or something. It's her way of communicating with them."

"I don't understand," Shullat said.

"I told you before old friend, my mother was once a Goddess. She sat upon the clouds in the sky with the other Gods and Goddesses. But somehow, it just wasn't fulfilling enough for her. She wished to have a child. She wished to experience the flesh, the simple joys that humans enjoy each day."

Shullat was listening intently, like a child to a bedtime story. "Then one day she saw my father from above," Gilgamesh continued. "He was a wise and powerful King, more righteous than any man before him. She came down and seduced him to have a child; an heir."

"That was you, right?" Shullat asked. Gilgamesh chuckled and leaned against the palace wall.

"Yes Shullat; that was me. Afterward, she ascended to the sky with me in her arms, and prepared me for my birthright. Dumuzi was a general for my father, and when my father had grown older and weaker, he and his sympathizers drove him from power! My father fled, and has not been seen since."

"Is he alive then?" Shullat asked. Gilgamesh looked at him, and then shook his head.

"Nobody knows. Some people believe him dead. Some people say that he was granted eternal life from the Gods for his righteousness, right before he was to die, and that he still wanders the land somewhere in the North. Still others say he was taken up into the clouds to become a God himself."

"Does your mother not know what happened?" inquired Shullat. Gilgamesh gave a vacant stare.

"She won't say," he responded. Then he stood straight and his tone became more serious. "It doesn't matter anyway general. What matters now is why my mother is acting so strange. I think it has something to do with a vision she had before."

"What vision?" Shullat asked Gilgamesh, raising an eyebrow.

"A vision of a man; someone who would challenge my authority and rival me in strength!"

"There is no such man that is as strong as you," Shullat laughed. "What I have seen you do, I have never seen any man, no matter how strong, do." Gilgamesh smiled and put his hand on Shullat's shoulder.

"This is true General," he said. "But my mother is never wrong about these things. She told me the man was sent by the Gods themselves as a balance to my power and dominance."

"Why would they do that Lord?" Shullat asked, scratching his head. Gilgamesh paused for a moment, and then turned away from Shullat.

"Because my mother said that my own subjects cried out for it!" he replied angrily, pounding his fist into the wall, and then quickly walked away. Shullat looked at the gaping hole that Gilgamesh had left with his fist in the wall; then he looked at the door to Nininsina's chamber for a moment.

Shullat walked back down to the armory, where Gilgamesh's army stored all of their weapons and armor for battle. He personally inspected all of the armor and weapons for Gilgamesh, making sure there were no defects or weakness in them. It was hardly necessary, as Dagon was an incredibly talented blacksmith and designer, but it was a matter of habit for Shullat; especially when there was something troubling on his mind.

What Gilgamesh had just told him was troubling. Shullat was young, but ambitious, and had never been loyal to any other King except for Gilgamesh, though he had served Dumuzi before him. He had been one of the few people in Dumuzi's army to remain with Gilgamesh after Dumuzi's defeat. He was short, but powerful and quick. Shullat was not educated or book smart, but his knowledge of battle and foresight for strategy in war was exceptional. That is why Gilgamesh chose him for General, and why they had become fast friends besides. He trusted Shullat more than anyone except Shamhat and his mother, and now that Shamhat had gone missing, he had relied on both Siduri and Shullat to confide in.

Shullat slowly walked past the racks of weapons, inspecting each one. But his thoughts were really fixed on Gilgamesh. There were many things that he did not tell him because of his new preoccupation with Siduri, and his worry over his mother. There were several people in the Kingdom that had become weary of Gilgamesh, though none would ever dare challenge him publicly. Gilgamesh had brought prosperity and security, but at the cost of freedom to his subjects. At first, they welcomed it after the rule of Dumuzi, whose Kingship had been rather loose and weak. He was nearly beaten by an Assyrian uprising of his own early in his rule, and again when he was battling the Egyptians over Southwestern territorial boundaries. Gilgamesh had usurped Dumuzi quite easily, and then quickly quelled any doubt of his power by handily beating back the Egyptians and Assyrians with his new army, which he personally led. But after a decade of rule, the people had become tired of his iron fist approach. To top matters off, there was talk from some people that the Egyptians were beginning to build an army again, possibly to overcome Gilgamesh and conquer Uruk. There was even talk of them forming an alliance with the Assyrians to dethrone Gilgamesh. These prospects gave Shullat a headache just thinking about them. And now his mother predicting his defeat from a man sent from the Gods? One could have a stroke just trying to handle the pressure he was now under to keep morale with the troops, quell public discourse, and possibly prepare again for war with the Egyptians!

Out on his favorite dune, Gilgamesh stared out at the sunset, as he often did when he was troubled. There was a feeling in the pit of his stomach. He wasn't sure what it was, but it was real and troubling. Gilgamesh had never been afraid of anything in his life. He had never had any reason to be. His mother had raised him with the belief he was invincible; a God, even if only in part. He had handily dispatched all challenges from opponents quite easily, and had never even been close to being equaled in strength, skill, or ingenuity. But now, all of that was in question. And to make it worse, it was his own mother predicting his possible downfall. The woman who had curried him to be the mightiest ruler in the history of the world was now, seemingly anyway, having doubts about the longevity of his reign. It worried him, and yes, even scared him a little bit. It was a strange feeling to be afraid, or even anxious about anything, but he was anxious about the coming encounter with this man from the vision. Worse yet, he didn't even know when it was coming. Nininsina had not given him a timetable, just a prediction of the near future.

Despite his feeling of trepidation, he knew that he must face the challenge, from whoever it was, with courage. This man had been sent by the Gods to be his equal balance; that is what his mother had told him anyway, whatever that meant. One thing was for sure, it would be the fight of his life, and he must prepare for it with every ounce of his strength. And he would be ready, he told himself; that much this challenger could count on!

While Gilgamesh was still deeply ingrained in his thoughts, Nininsina had come out from her chamber, and stood next to him on the dune. The sky was glowing with the colors of sunset, purple and shades of red. She put her hand on his shoulder, arousing him from his daydreaming state.

"It is about time mother," Gilgamesh stated rather blandly toward her. She gave a faint smile. Her cheeks were sunken in from lack of eating, and her face quite pale. Gilgamesh turned to her and stared at her face long and hard.

"You look very ill mother," he said, now with a bit more concern than before.

"I have been busy, communing with the Gods," she told him. It seemed to take a great deal of effort to even speak. Gilgamesh put his hand on her shoulder.

"And what have the Gods told you?" he asked her with beaming curiosity. He was very anxious to find out what his mother might know about his approaching fate. Nininsina took a deep breath to catch her wind before speaking again.

"I have seen many things in my visions from the Gods," she said. "The impending fight is rapidly approaching, and you must prepare. You must prepare for a battle like no other you have ever faced my Son." The seriousness of her tone was apparent.

Gilgamesh turned from his mother. He gazed into the sky for a moment before turning back to Nininsina. "What happens if I lose Mother?" he asked her. Nininsina was silent for a moment. He turned back to her and looked her in her eyes. "Please Mother, I must know! What happens to me, my Kingdom?"

"I don't know Gilgamesh," she stated.

"But you know everything Mother! You are, after all, a Goddess!" Gilgamesh blustered. Nininsina took another deep breath.

"There are some things that even I cannot foresee my son," she told him. She turned from him and began to hobble back toward the palace. Gilgamesh followed closely behind.

"What is it Mother? What aren't you telling me?"

"I cannot interfere with destiny or fate Gilgamesh," she said as she continued slowly walking. "Some things *must* happen, and they must happen for a reason. I cannot interfere. It's one of the oldest pacts that the Gods made before the beginning of time."

"Come now Mother," Gilgamesh began," the Gods interject themselves into human life everywhere. They command them to build temples, statues. They command them to worship, bring offerings. When they disobey, they cause floods, storms, and pestilence. Why is this any different?"

Nininsina stopped and slowly turned toward her Son. "The Gods only interject themselves for the good of their subjects," she told him flatly. Gilgamesh looked unconvinced. Nininsina went on, "Humans are like children. They need to be given rules to survive. It is in their nature to destroy themselves; to bicker, quarrel, and fight each other selfishly for things that are abundant in the world such as land, cattle, and gold. Without the Gods' rules to give them a moral compass, they will not survive!"

"I still don't understand why...." Gilgamesh started to say. Nininsina put her hand up to stop him.

"You don't have to understand right now my son," she told him. "After all, if humans understood everything, they would be Gods, wouldn't they?"

"I *am* also part God," Gilgamesh reminded her. Nininsina nodded. "Why then do the Gods not merely subject people to their will?"

"It is true that we could make humans conform to anything we wish. But would that be any different than slavery? The Gods do not wish to enslave humans. If that's what we wanted, we could have done it ages ago. We want humans to worship us of their own choosing. It is the only satisfying relationship we would have with our creation; our children. Humans need to be able to choose right from wrong. Only then is choosing to do the right thing of any value to us, or them. They are our children, and we love them, protect them, and cherish them. And we wish them to love us in return; not because we forced them to, but because *they* wish to show their gratitude for the beautiful world and many good things we have created for them." Gilgamesh listened intently to his mother as she spoke, but he was still filled with questions.

"I still don't see why you can't tell me *exactly* what is to come? What would it hurt in the grand scheme of the universe?" Gilgamesh said with a sarcastic tone. Nininsina glared back at her son, then lifted her hand and slapped him across the face. Gilgamesh was stunned. She had never laid a finger on him before!

"My son, I came down from the heavens to be with your father and conceive a King who would be the most powerful ruler in the world!" Nininsina fumed. "One who would bring peace and prosperity to all of Sumeria in the name of the Gods, after I witnessed King after King destroy humanity with his greed and lust for power! And what have you done with your Kingdom? You have instilled fear in your subjects, conquered peaceful nations, raped women, enslaved the Assyrians, provoked the Egyptians, and now shown disrespect to me; the one who ensured your power and life of privilege!" Nininsina was struggling to breathe as she vented her frustrations at her Son, but she continued anyway. Gilgamesh tried to put his hand on her shoulder, but she knocked it away. "You are not a beacon of the Gods in this world as I had hoped. You are a ruthless dictator who enjoys subjugating your people to a life of terror! It is not the reason you were to be my son!" Nininsina was wheezing now as she spoke. Gilgamesh put his hand on her shoulder, but she brushed it away again.

"Mother, please," he begged. "You are not in condition to do this! You could die in your weakened state!"

"Then let me die," she said to him blankly. She turned away from him again and struggled to walk back toward the palace. "It is time I left this mortal body anyway. The eve of my return to the heavens is upon me. I have done everything I could for you in your life, and now it is time for me to go." Gilgamesh stood motionless, his mouth open and speechless. Nininsina stopped and turned back toward her son for a moment. "The one who will change your life forever will soon be coming for you Gilgamesh," she told him, "and you must prepare. It is destined to be. I cannot interfere with it for the good of your people; and you!"

Gilgamesh watched his mother drag herself back to the palace doors, coughing and wheezing all the way. Then she disappeared inside. He felt empty. It was all too much to absorb at one time. He had never argued with his mother before, and she had never been so harsh toward him. Gilgamesh walked back to the dune where he was standing before. The sky had gone dark and he could see the stars shining in the heavens above. There was a cold wind blowing, but Gilgamesh didn't care. It could not possibly be as cold as he already felt inside tonight.

----------------------------------------------------------------------

Shamhat waited patiently for her host to reappear. He had abruptly left her after catching her dinner. It had been several hours now, and she was beginning to believe he might not return. Perhaps she should try to find a way out of the forest. It might be her last chance to escape.

However, she wasn't entirely sure she where the way out was; or, for that matter, if she wanted to. That was her quandary. She was somehow drawn to this man. He was an animal, essentially, but just as she had been drawn to the forest with Adad in the first place, she felt as though there was a reason for her being there now.

Her thoughts were interrupted by a loud thud maybe 20 or 30 feet away. Out of the darkness, the man approached her again. This time though, Shamhat didn't flinch at the sight of him. He was carrying a deer on his back, obviously meant as another gift for her. Dropping it to the ground, he came toward her. This time, Shamhat didn't try to run. Doing so would be futile anyways, but it was more than that. As she watched him walk closer to her, she felt herself a bit excited by him. It was sudden and powerful, but she felt herself suddenly attracted to him like she had never been with any other; not even Gilgamesh. The feeling was inexplicable, but it was there nonetheless.

The man stepped very close to her; close enough that she could feel his breath on her neck. Her heart was racing, and she could tell that his was also. It was beginning to remind her of the feelings she experienced in the dream she had. The animal-like man was breathing heavily and seemed for the first time to be unsure of what he was doing, almost confused. She knew that he felt as strongly attracted to her as she was to him. She could see it in his eyes, the same look of lust that she had seen with so many men before. Shamhat leaned forward and quickly kissed him on the cheek. The man didn't move, but seemed to almost sigh as a smile broke out across his face.

Shamhat stepped back a few paces and stared into his eyes. She grinned devilishly at him. He seemed to like the way she was looking at him, and he smiled and let out a grunt. Undoing the traditional sleeveless robe that all Sumerian women wore from the left shoulder, she let her covering drop to the ground. At once, the man's eyes became as wide as a canyon and his breathing became more notable and fast. Shamhat was enjoying the moment. It was the first time since he brought her there that she felt she was in her element and in control. It didn't matter where a man lived or how, he was still a man, she thought to herself. She could still control him as any other with her body and cunning.

The wild man slowly inched toward her as she stretched out her arms to welcome him. She could see he was very cautious, but he couldn't resist coming to her arms. When he was so close to her, she grabbed him and kissed him on the lips. At first he was confused and pulled away. Shamhat gazed at him lustily, and he again came slowly to her. She kissed him again passionately. This time he did not pull away as he was seemingly enjoying it. The man grabbed Shamhat and threw her over his shoulder. He carried her over to the base of a large tree and set her down on her back. The rest seemed to come naturally to the man, though she was sure he had never had made love to a woman before. He was wild and uncontrolled; and Shamhat loved it! They made love over and over for six days and seven nights, only briefly stopping in between when he left to fetch some water.

At the end of the seventh night, Shamhat was laying beside the man. She was exhausted, but as happy as she had been in a very long time. Though she loved Gilgamesh, or at least lusted after him and his power, she had never experienced the rawness and the unbridled carnal desires she felt with this man. Surely he was sent to her from the Gods, she thought to herself. Gazing over at the man, who was also exhausted and now sleeping, she leaned over and kissed him on his cheek. Slowly opening his eyes, the man looked at her and smiled.

"I know you can't understand me," she whispered to him, "but I think I love you!" The man lifted his head and sat up, looking confused.

"But I do understand you!" he said to her with a huge grin on his face. Shamhat was astonished. Her eyes grew wide in amazement when she heard him speak.

"You can understand me?" she asked him, shaking her head.

"Yes," he replied. Shamhat was still dazed.

"How?"

"I don't quite know," he said, still rather unsure of what was happening himself. "I don't know why, but suddenly, I can understand everything you say to me! Before when you spoke, it was just....gibberish. But now, I know what you are saying when you speak! And you can understand me as well?"

Shamhat nodded her head, and then smiled the biggest smile she had ever had in her life. She flung her arms around the man so hard that she knocked him down on the ground. Both of them were laughing in delight at their newfound connection.

"Surely it is a gift from the Gods that you can understand me!" Shamhat said gleefully.

"Yes, it must be," he happily acknowledged.

"Tell me love," she began, "how did you come to live in the forest with all of the animals?"

"I'm not really sure," he told her, standing up and pacing in front of her. "The first thing I can ever remember is running through the forest as any other animal. Everything felt natural. I have lived among the forest animals in complete harmony ever since."

"How long have you been here? Do you know?" she asked. He thought for a moment, and then shook his head.

"I really can't say," he said. "It seems like an eternity though; as though I have always been here."

Shamhat smiled and looked up to the sky. "It is the will of the Gods that you are here with me now my love," she told him.

"What do you mean?" he queried. Shamhat stood up and took his hands in hers.

"There is a great city to the south of this forest. It is called Uruk, and it is where the King of all the land of Sumeria lives. His name is Gilgamesh, and for some time, his subjects have been praying for relief from his tyranny!"

"I don't understand," he said, scratching his head in confusion. "What does this have to do with me?"

"I believe that the Gods have heard the prayers of the suffering people of Uruk," Shamhat told him. He continued to stare at her with a blank look on his face. Shamhat rolled her eyes. "That relief is you my love!"

"Me?" he answered.

"Yes, you! I am certain of it!"

"Why me?"

"Because I can tell you truthfully," Shamhat said to him, "that there is no other man like King Gilgamesh in all of the land. I have never seen anyone of such strength and fighting ability; of such wisdom and cunning. He himself is part God, the son of the Goddess Nininsina. There is no one who can challenge him in battle."

"No one?" he asked her.

Shamhat smiled. "That is, except for you my love!"

The man opened his eyes wide and shook his head. "I cannot fight him," he told her. Shamhat's demeanor immediately changed.

"Why not!?" Shamhat snapped back at him.

"It is not in my nature to fight," he told her.

"Don't be ridiculous," she said to him, smirking. "When you first brought me here, I saw you rip apart a bird to feed me! And don't tell me that if you encountered a lion, bear, or something vicious, you would not hesitate to fight it?"

"Only for defense and survival," he told her. "I was created to be one with nature here. I am like the animals. Animals are not like the humans. They do not kill or murder for the glory of battle, to conquer or settle old scores, or even to make kingdoms with boundaries and borders they must always defend. They live in peace and respect with one another. I cannot be involved in the way of humans. My life is here, in the forest with my brother animals."

Shamhat was beginning to wonder if she was really pleased to hear him speak after all. At first she had wished that he could understand her and talk to her, now she wished he would be silent. He was living like an animal not days before, now he spoke as though he wanted to become a great philosopher or something! She stared at him as he spoke with irritation in her eyes, and he was beginning to notice it the more he spoke.

"Listen to me my love," Shamhat told him, changing her tactics a bit, "please trust in me that you are here by the Gods. I saw you in a vision and was drawn here by the will of the Goddess Ishtar. Why else would I be out here, so far from civilization, if not for you my love?" The man looked at her and shrugged his shoulders. "It is only for you that I am here. And it is only for the people of Uruk that the Gods have sent you. So many of them are suffering, and you are the only one who can stop Gilgamesh. Is there not a more noble reason to do battle than to save others from oppression and pain?"

It was hard to argue with her logic. "I suppose not," he whispered, looking down at the ground and shaking his head. Shamhat smiled. She was beginning to see him sway to her side, and she was ecstatic with the thought of this man usurping the great and powerful Gilgamesh. It would serve him right after the pain he had caused her!

All of her life she wished for power. She had been abandoned by her father when she was just twelve, and had been forced to live in the street, scavenging the waste of other farmers and townspeople to have something to eat. She never knew her mother, and her father refused to speak of her. She had finally been "rescued" by Gilgamesh when she was 15, and she had vowed at that time that she would rise to greatness. At first, she wished she could be the high priestess of the temple of Ishtar. Then she had longed and fantasized for many years that she could be close enough to Gilgamesh that he would someday take her for her Queen, only to be disappointed and blocked by his mother time and time again. No, his mother was not the only one. Gilgamesh himself treated her as a toy to be played with whenever he pleased! Now, she was beginning to realize that there was another path to power; one that she had never anticipated. One that she was sure she was destined for. The proof was that she was led here by nothing more than blind faith in her vision, and kept alive by the will of The Gods. It had to have been provided by the Gods that she would find this man and bring him back to Uruk to fight Gilgamesh, and after his downfall, he would be the new ruler of all Sumeria; and she would be his Queen!

"The first thing we need to do is find you some clothes," she told him. The man looked at her a bit bewildered.

"Why?" he bluntly asked her.

"You must wear clothing! You cannot run around naked like an animal if you are to live with people now," she reasoned. The man didn't seem to like the sound of that. He had never worn anything in his life. There was no need. His thick hair had always kept him warm in the cold of the nights like a bear, and there would be no more ridiculous a sight than to see a bear with sandals and a robe!

"I don't want to wear clothing," muttered the man. Shamhat cocked her head to one side and stared at him. Then she smiled, and moved close to him. She put her hand on his manhood and kissed him passionately on the lips. She could feel it rising as she kissed him.

"Will you not do this for me my love!" she cooed into his ear. The man closed his eyes and sighed in pleasure as she caressed him.

"I will do as you ask," he replied. Shamhat smiled and threw her arms around him. She couldn't help but chuckle to herself privately. So powerful, yet so weak, she thought to herself. Whether God or mortal, men were all the same!

---

Siduri lay sprawled out on Gilgamesh's bed. She was worried; worried about him. Since his mother had fought with Gilgamesh, he had been a wreck. The once brash, arrogant, and cocky ruler had been reduced to an almost childlike state. His mother was the only one who could do that.

Nininsina was close to death. Everyone knew it, especially Gilgamesh. Without his mother to guide him, he began to feel lost and disoriented. He had assumed that she would never die. After all, she was a Goddess. He had always taken for granted that she would always be there to be his counsel in all decisions. And what was worse, was it seemed in these last days that she had grown quite disappointed in him. That was the real stake through the heart for Gilgamesh. He had always been the proverbial apple of his mother's eye. Now it seemed she had abandoned her support for him. As the days went on since they had last argued, Nininsina had not left her chamber, nor had she eaten a thing. Gilgamesh was fraught with worry, but there was nothing he could do. The all powerful King was helpless to convince his mother that she must eat and take care of her health. It seemed that she wanted to die!

Siduri had just drifted off to sleep when she was awoken by a loud noise. It was the sound of the chamber door being flung open and hitting the wall behind it. Gilgamesh stepped into his room from outside. She sat up from the bed to see someone standing in the doorway. The only light was the dim candlelight coming from the hallway outside the room, which made his silhouette the only clear thing visible. Siduri could tell it was him though from his outline. She knew every inch of his body well. He was dressed in his Golden military armor. Perhaps he had just come from drills with Shullat and his warriors, Siduri surmised. But there was something wrong. As Gilgamesh slowly began to walk forward toward the window on the opposite side of the room, she could begin to make out his face. It was pale as he stared into the darkness of the room in a zombie like trance. He didn't seem to notice Siduri laying there on the bed, as he passed right by her without a word or even glance.

Gilgamesh walked over to the window and stopped. Putting one hand on the window sill, he gazed out into the garden that was directly below his chamber. Beyond the garden he could see great wall he had built surrounding Uruk. And beyond that was nothing to be seen for miles beyond the city. Once there had been many wooden homes and farmers living near Uruk, but

Gilgamesh had ordered all the farmers executed and their homes burnt to the ground after taking power. There were a great many of the people who had vocally loved and supported Dumuzi, even after it became apparent he would lose the throne to Gilgamesh, and Gilgamesh decided it best to make examples of those people, to inhibit any thought of rebellion against him. But looking out at the ruins of burnt homes and desolation outside the great wall now, he had the chilling feeling that he may be headed for the same fate as Dumuzi. Perhaps his time had come, as Dumuzi's had come when Gilgamesh challenged him. He just didn't know anymore.

Siduri got up from the bed and walked over to Gilgamesh, staring out at the vastness of his Kingdom from his window. She put her one hand on his shoulder, and the other on his back, massaging it up and down. He didn't even seem to notice.

"I was worried about you my Lord," Siduri whispered to Gilgamesh. He didn't answer, nor even turn his head. She continued to massage his back, and then she moved her hands to his neck to massage that.

"Siduri," Gilgamesh whispered. She stopped massaging and walked to his side so she could see his face.

"Yes my Lord," she answered. Gilgamesh paused for a moment before responding.

"She's gone," he said meekly.

"Who is gone?" she queried.

"My mother," he replied. His expression never changed and his eyes never left the gaze out the window.

"Your mother?" Siduri said in disbelief. Gilgamesh nodded, still turned from her. "I don't believe it!"

"It's true," he flatly answered. Siduri rested her head against his shoulder.

"I'm so sorry Gilgamesh," she told him. "If there is anything I can do for you?"

"No, there is nothing."

"Are you sure?" Siduri asked again.

Gilgamesh turned and faced Siduri. He took her hands in his and looked into her eyes for a moment. It was a bit awkward for her. She wasn't sure what he was thinking. Finally, Gilgamesh uttered just four words to her; "Can I trust you?" Siduri was a bit stunned by the question. She felt as though she had already completely demonstrated her loyalty to the King. The question took her by surprise, and also stung her ego a bit.

"Of course you can trust me," she told him. "Have I ever done anything to make you think otherwise?"

"No," Gilgamesh said. He pulled his hands away from hers and walked toward the chamber door. "I must prepare for battle now." His actions and questions were quite peculiar, and Siduri was becoming very worried.

"Gilgamesh?" she called after him. He continued to walk to the door, not answering. Siduri could feel her heart racing. She wasn't sure why he had asked her this question, or suddenly turned cold towards her. Gilgamesh stopped at the entrance of the doorway and slowly turned back toward Siduri.

"Just remember," he began, "I don't like to be betrayed. And if I ever find that I have been betrayed….." Gilgamesh paused a moment and stared down at the floor. "…..well, there is no worse fate for anyone than this." Gilgamesh looked back up into Siduri's eyes from across the room then closed the chamber door behind him. Siduri sat, stunned at what she was hearing. What could he mean by this? She would never betray him. It all seemed like a bad dream; a nightmare, really. It made her sick to her stomach. Suddenly, she felt a sharp pain. Siduri doubled over as the pain became unbearable. Then, just as quickly, she felt sick to her stomach. She wanted to vomit. It was too far to the royal bath, so she stuck her head out of the window and let it go. Hopefully there was no one right below her, she thought. She sat down on the bed after the wave of sickness was gone, but still panting heavily as though she had been running. Her head was dizzy, so she lay back on the bed and closed her eyes. The room felt as though it was spinning.

"What is going on?" she whispered to herself, weakly. She had never felt so sick in all her life. It must be what he had said to her, she thought. Being as sensitive as she was, it truly made her sick to think he couldn't trust her; and then to even threaten her as though she were a common criminal! She didn't understand, but all she could do at the moment was sleep. She felt exhausted, her stomach was still upset, and the room was still spinning. What a day it had been! Siduri couldn't possibly imagine what would be next.

Gilgamesh mounted his horse and prepared to ride out to his favorite dune. Tomorrow he would have to lead his army against the Assyrian uprising. They had formed a makeshift camp just a several miles away from the outer wall of the city, he had learned from one of his spies who had joined them to monitor their activities. The uprising had been brewing for some time, and Gilgamesh had ordered Shullat to prepare all of his troops for battle, and had commissioned several more socket axes, body armor, and sickle swords to be made by Dagon. Though Dagon hated Gilgamesh, he continued to do as he asked because of his daughter.

Slowly riding out toward the dune that lay just beyond the great wall, he was suddenly accosted by an older man. The man came out of nowhere and began shouting at him.

"You piece of filth! There is no one that the Gods despise more than you Gilgamesh! You're not a God as they say you are; you're just a bastard! I curse your name and pray the Gods destroy you! As we suffer and starve, you parade about the city in your Gold armor and fancy garments! Death be to you Gilgamesh! Death be to you!"

Gilgamesh had sat on his horse, amusedly listening to the old man berate him. Then, finally, when he had had enough, he drew his sword and swung. The old man's head fell, rolling to the ground. Gilgamesh wiped the blood from his shiny sword, and put it back in its sheath, and rode out toward the dune once again. He sighed heavily as he reached the top of the dune, and stared out at the reddish tint of the sky as the sun set. There would be hundreds of those crazy old men tomorrow; maybe thousands. Though they would be just as easy to kill and silence, Gilgamesh began to wonder about things to come. Not the Assyrians, they were nothing more than a quick mosquito swat from defeat. But the words from his mother's lips still bothered him. The dreams and visions she had about a challenger from the Gods still weighed on his mind. On this night, the dune didn't seem quite as beautiful or comforting as it had been in the past.

# TABLET TWO

*"That which is given in submission becomes a medium of defiance..............."*

It was a small shack, but it was still shelter; better than living nowhere. Still, the roof had small holes that leaked when it rained, and the floor simply consisted of old straw mats that had been put down to cover the sand. Shamhat found it to be nearly unlivable, but she endured it. It would only be a matter of time before Enkidu would be ready to blend in with people completely, she told herself. Then she could take him to Uruk, and finally have the revenge she sought; and ultimately, the power she craved.

With his son murdered, and his wife long dead, Adad had grown a bit crazy in his isolation. It hadn't done him any good to have seen Enkidu that day when he had led Shamhat to the forest either. It seemed to tip him over the edge into insanity. Day and night he sat in the corner of the house, mumbling incoherently to himself, and rocking back and forth. Shamhat cooked him food and fed him as if he were an infant. When they had arrived, the farm which he lived on had been untended for some time, and there

117

were no crops anywhere to be found. All the ones that had been there had vanished without care. Enkidu took up the job of replanting the crops for Adad in return for a place to stay. Without their help, Adad would have surely died of starvation.

With what little things were left in the home, Shamhat prepared breakfast for the three of them. Using barley, she made small cakes. With what little wheat there was, she was able to make some bread, and with what vegetables had not become rotten, she had made some salad. It wouldn't be long, though, before all the food in the home was gone. Shamhat hoped that they could last until new crops came in from Enkidu's efforts. If not, they would all wind up starving!

Adad's home was kind of secluded. It was at least two miles away from any other home, so there were no neighbors to look after him or help in any way; at least, not on a daily basis. There had been a few people here and there that had dropped by to see how he was, but that was it. Shamhat wondered why he had chosen such a remote spot to build a home. It was a bit odd. He and his son would have to travel at least five miles to come to the edge of the forest where Enkidu had been living, where they had trapped rabbits and small animals for food, and where both fresh and salt water could be found for drinking and fishing. She had tried to ask him the reason before, when she had first come out there, but he had never really answered her. He just danced around the question.

Enkidu came through the doorway of the Adad's home and smiled at Shamhat. She returned the gesture, and motioned for him to sit on the large mat in the middle of the floor. It was where they sat to eat their meals; except for Adad that is. He sat day and night in the corner of the adjoining room, rocking back and forth while speaking what sounded like gibberish. Neither Shamhat nor Enkidu could ever seem to make out any cogent thought from what he was saying. Nevertheless, day and night he sat there. Shamhat would bring his food and set it at his feet. Sometimes she would come back an hour later, and it was still there; sometimes not. Adad seemed to eat just enough to live, yet not enough to be healthy in appearance or thought.

"I'm starved," Enkidu told Shamhat as he sat down.

"I hope that the crops you planted come in soon," she worriedly told him. "Every meal I have to make less and less. Soon there will be nothing left to eat for any of us."

"Don't worry," Enkidu told her. "If it be the will of the Gods that we starve, then we starve. But I don't think that will happen. As you said, I have come to live with people for a reason. I don't believe the Gods will let us die here." Shamhat smiled and nodded.

"Perhaps you are right," she sighed. Then her mood turned darker in almost an instant. "Still, it's a far cry from the life I was living just a few months ago. In Uruk, I was living in the royal palace and was personal consort to the King himself. Now look at me! Dressed in these dirty clothes and cooking tiny meals of wheat and barley!" she raged. She put her hands on her hips and let out a groan. "Sometimes I wonder why I came here," she told Enkidu. She began to stir the contents of the clay bowl she was working in, and then, in a fit, Shamhat threw it against the wall. The bowl shattered, and the contents lied scattered on the floor. Enkidu raised an eyebrow and stared at her as she pounded the wall and shook her head; then she bent down and proceeded to pick up the shattered pieces.

"Is this the manner in which I should act?" Enkidu asked Shamhat with a smirk on his face, referring to her tantrum. Shamhat looked over at him, then shook her head and continued to clean up the mess.

Sometimes he grew weary of Shamhat's constant complaining of her "glamorous" life in the palace. Life had to be about much more than that or she wouldn't have been led by the Goddess to his forest in the first place. Shamhat admitted as much, but still pined day and night about her situation. He assured her it would get better. The Gods would make it better in time. For the moment though, she had been teaching him valuable things about how to be around people. It was important he learn these simple things before he returned to Uruk with her. Enkidu was certain that the Gods had a plan for making him. He was unique; shaped like an ordinary man, but containing the traits of the animals. It would make no sense otherwise than he was born to be something important.

There were times, though, that he questioned Shamhat's motives. He had a feeling deep down that the only reason she wanted him to challenge Gilgamesh was a lust for power. Enkidu could see it in her eyes when she talked about him becoming King if he defeated Gilgamesh. The only other time he saw that look was during intercourse, but only sometimes. When she spoke of Gilgamesh's downfall, she *always* had that look. Of course, she would also add that he could rule the Kingdom freely, and bring peace and justice to all the people who had been oppressed by Gilgamesh. There was probably truth to that, but it seemed that there was more to it than that for Shamhat. Anyway, he had trouble saying "no" to her from the beginning. All it seemed she had to do was kiss him or touch him in a certain way, and his animal side would come out and they would make love. After, he would always wind up doing whatever she asked anyhow. Enkidu was sure she noticed this pattern too, and often used it to get what she wanted from him. Still, he couldn't seem to resist her no matter how much he tried.

Suddenly, Adad came bursting through the doorway to the other room where he sat all day. He knocked Shamhat down as he raced by, headed for the doorway outside. Enkidu leapt to his feet with the agility and speed of a cat, and grabbed him from behind.

"What in the world are you doing Adad?" he asked him, holding him up in the air. Adad's feet were still moving, as if he were unaware that they weren't on the ground anymore. Finally, after a moment, Adad stopped his running motion, and Enkidu put him back down on the floor. Wild-eyed and panting, Adad's eyes scanned the room. He appeared as if he were looking for something.

Enkidu looked over at Shamhat, who shrugged her shoulders and shook her head. "What are you looking for Adad? Perhaps I can help?"

"I've got to find her!" he exclaimed nervously. He began to ransack the room, overturning mats on the floor, throwing plates and cooking utensils around. "I've got to save her!" Adad shouted. Enkidu grabbed him from behind again, to stop him before he destroyed the entire house.

"Who? Who do you have to find old man?" Shamhat shouted at him, becoming a bit irritated. Adad didn't answer. He kept fighting Enkidu to try to free himself, but it was a useless effort for him to even try.

"Come on Adad," Enkidu told him, "Who do you have to find. You can tell us, we're your friends, remember?" Adad stopped struggling for a moment. He turned his head and looked at Enkidu. Then he turned his head to the other side and looked at Shamhat. With a confused look in his eyes, he began to shake his head.

"Where am I?" he asked to Shamhat. Adad turned and looked at Enkidu. "Who are you?" he asked him. Shamhat cocked her head to one side and stared back at him for a moment before answering.

"My name is Shamhat," she said. Adad still stood with a dazed look. "Don't you remember me?" Adad didn't answer. Shamhat inched toward him slowly. He didn't move, just put his hand on his head and shook it. "Adad, don't you remember me at all?"

"No," he replied softly, still confused as to who these strangers were in his home. Then he turned his head again slowly, and stared at Enkidu for a moment. Suddenly, his eyes grew wide.

"You!" he shouted, jumping quickly away from Enkidu and crouching into a corner. "I know you!"

"Yes," Enkidu told him, putting his hands up. "I am Enkidu, and she is Shamhat," he said, pointing in her direction. "We came to stay with you because you took ill."

"No!" Adad shouted back. "You've come to take her!"

"What are you talking about?" Enkidu asked him.

"You're from *HIM*, and you've come to take her away from me!" he shouted.

"Take who away?" Shamhat asked Adad. He didn't acknowledge her at all, just kept his eyes fixed on Enkidu.

"I will die before I let you harm her!" he screamed at Enkidu. Quickly, Adad jumped up and ran as fast as he could out the front opening of the home. Enkidu looked over at Shamhat for a moment, wondering if he should follow. Shamhat stood with her mouth wide open, stunned by Adad's sudden burst of energy and odd behavior. Enkidu rushed out the door to catch Adad. He found him standing by a small bush near the back of the home. He could see Adad bending down and digging for something. Enkidu started over toward him, when Adad turned quickly around to face him. It suddenly became clear what Adad was after, and he had found it. The rusted tip of the blade was pointed right at Enkidu's chest. It was an old sword. Adad must have hidden it there long ago, well before they had arrived. He wasn't sure why, but it didn't matter. Right now he was pointing the sword at him in a quite menacing way. Adad brought the sword back, and then swung at Enkidu as hard as he could.

"I won't let you kill them!" he shouted at Enkidu as he swung at him over and over. He hit nothing but air. Enkidu was already gone by the time he had finished each of his swings, moving as quickly as a rabbit out of the path of the sword. Then Enkidu leapt into the air. Adad looked up, then from side to side, wondering where he had gone. His search was soon ended by the tap of a finger on his shoulder. He turned around to find Enkidu behind him. Adad raised the sword again, but Enkidu quickly knocked it away from him and lifted him by the neck into the air. Adad put both his hands onto Enkidu's wrist and tried to pry his grip away, but to no avail. He was much too strong for Adad. Adad began to weep.

"Please, you can kill me if you wish. Do anything to me you wish, but just don't hurt her," he sobbed. Enkidu slowly brought Adad's feet back to the ground and released his grip. Adad collapsed on the ground and continued to cry and grovel. "It's burning….It's burning! My little girl is burning!" Adad repeated, tears gushing from his eyes.

"I don't understand Adad," Enkidu told him. "Who is this girl you are speaking of? And what is burning?" Adad was trying to fight back his tears as he spoke.

"My…..My daughter, I must save her" he said, tears streaming down his cheeks. Enkidu stood and looked at Adad. He wasn't aware he had a daughter. He had been told by Shamhat about what had happened to Agga, his son, in Uruk by the palace guards, but she had never mentioned a daughter. Just at that moment, Shamhat cautiously came walking outside to see what was happening.

"Do you know what he's talking about Shamhat?" Enkidu asked her.

"What do you mean?" she replied, scrunching her face up. Adad was sitting on the ground now, his face buried in his hands.

"He says he has a daughter, and that he has to protect her from someone," Enkidu told her. Shamhat shook her head, bewildered.

"He never told me anything," she said. "But, then again, there is much we don't know about this man. I only met him in Uruk before coming to find you. I helped him because he was locked up and dying after they murdered his son. I never even thought to ask him if he had any other children."

"Well, apparently he does. Or, at least, he thinks he does," Enkidu said.

"Come back inside," she said to Enkidu, taking his arm and pulling. Enkidu resisted her.

"We should not just leave him outside like this," he told her.

"You need to eat, and so do I," she said to him. "He is too far gone to even reason with now. Just leave him be until he comes to his senses and comes back inside." Enkidu looked at Shamhat and shook his head.

"No, I will not leave him here. This is his house after all, and we are his guests, whether he remembers us or not. We should take care of him until he is well."

"We don't have time to take care of him!" Shamhat shot back, suddenly changing the tone in her voice. "You and I must travel to Uruk in two days, before the setting of the full moon. Certainly nothing has changed in the few months I have been gone, and at every full moon, Gilgamesh will roam the town and look for a new girl for his brothel. He will be outside of the palace with only a few guards with him. It will be dark, and we will have the advantage of surprise; a perfect time to ambush and kill him!" Enkidu's expression turned to anger.

"First of all, I will not *ambush* anyone," Enkidu told Shamhat, now raising his voice back at her. He didn't care for the tone of her voice or her total lack of feeling for the life and well being of a fellow human. She seemed taken aback at his firmness. "If I am to fight the King, then it will be a fair fight for everyone to see. Secondly, we need to care for others who are in need. This is just as important as anything we can do to honor the Gods who made us!" Shamhat was steaming. Her eyes narrowed as the anger became apparent on her face as he was speaking. Then she decided it was useless to argue with him about it, and she stormed off back inside the house. Enkidu shook his head and turned back toward Adad. His head was still buried in his hands.

"Come Adad, let's go back inside," he said to him, holding out his hand. Adad didn't move. He rocked back and forth like he had done for so many days inside the house in an almost catatonic state. Enkidu walked over to him and picked him up easily, putting him over his shoulder, and carried him back into the house to have some dinner; at least, whatever was left after Shamhat's tantrum earlier. She had broken the one bowl full of barley she was mixing to make cakes, but there were still the vegetables for a salad and the bread. It was better than nothing.

Enkidu found Shamhat sitting on the floor, still shaking her head and mumbling to herself. She could be quite the volcano when she did not get her way, Enkidu thought to himself. Sometimes he wondered if she were any better than the picture she had so often painted of Gilgamesh to him. She always made him out to be an arrogant monster who controlled his subjects' lives at every turn, but wasn't that what she wanted as well? For that matter, maybe all humans were like this. It was still a foreign concept to Enkidu who had lived for so many years with the animals. Everything was shared there, each animal respecting the other. Even if they preyed on each other sometimes for food, they did so for survival, not greed. If this was how humans acted, maybe he wasn't interested in saving any of them after all!

But then again, he was still sure that everything happened for a reason, and there was still something in his heart that he knew he must do in Uruk. He felt it, as if it were programmed in him from the Gods. But whether it was to become King or something else, he couldn't say. He would have to wait for two more days to find out; at the setting of the next full moon.

-------------------------------------------------------------------------

The battle seemed endless. This was much more than Shullat and Gilgamesh had expected from them. Furiously blocking swords and knives with their golden shields, the two men stood back to back in the middle of the frenzy.

Gilgamesh's mastery of the sword and incredible strength helped him mow down the Assyrians one by one as they approached. Shullat as well, with his short, but incredibly strong physique, was able to easily defeat his less powerful opponents. But the enormous number of Assyrians was overwhelming. All around the two men lay the bodies of Gilgamesh's soldiers and horses from his scout brigade, many with spears still sticking in their sides, and various body parts strewn about. They had been ambushed and slaughtered before Gilgamesh and Shullat had arrived with their main force of troops. The Assyrians had assembled a massive army, though most were only equipped with poor quality swords, spears and knives, and no body armor or shields. They had hoped to simply envelop and overwhelm Gilgamesh's army. It was their only chance to win.

The well trained soldiers of Uruk had fought bravely, and killed many before they were overrun by the sheer number of Assyrian fighters, determined to overthrow Gilgamesh. Now with the main force of troops behind Gilgamesh and Shullat, they were pushing back the Assyrians. Yet it seemed that as they pushed back, more fighters began to appear from everywhere. It was evident that Gilgamesh's army was outnumbered by the Assyrians, but both Shullat and Gilgamesh knew they must be defeated here and now, or they would continue to gather support from more and more people outside the city of Uruk. It was also rumored that many of the weapons, food, and supplies had been given to them by Egyptian sympathizers. This was of great concern to Gilgamesh, as the Egyptians had a very well organized and trained army of their own. Relations between the two had been friendly for several years, but there had always been mistrust and tension between Gilgamesh and the new Pharaoh, Khasekhemwy.

But right now that concern would have to wait. Forming a solid line of soldiers behind them, Gilgamesh and Shullat charged straight into their weaker opponents for a few moments. The Assyrian fighters condensed into a singular crowd of fighters and advanced on the wall of Gilgamesh's soldiers. Then with a look over to Shullat and a nod in response, Gilgamesh quickly broke off to the left side of the battlefield on horseback with half of his soldiers, while Shullat led the other half to the right. The bright glow of the golden armor from Gilgamesh's soldiers shone brightly in the face of the Assyrians. Chopping their way through the lowly perimeter fighters, Gilgamesh and Shullat led their troops in a circular pattern, surrounding the much less organized Assyrians. Now with soldiers surrounding them, the Assyrians stood and looked at the surrounding soldiers of Uruk. On the hills east and west of them, they began to see more of Gilgamesh's army appearing seemingly out of nowhere, riding on chariots, each of them carrying a short spear and sword, and the dreaded socket axe that had been developed by Dagon. These axes could cut straight through body armor and shields, making such protection useless, and these special troops had been trained to even throw the axes with deadly accuracy.

Gilgamesh's troops on chariots began to throw the axes with the greatest of precision at the stream of Assyrian fighters that were left outside of the encircled main force. In an instant, Gilgamesh's cavalry had killed several dozens of straggling Assyrians on the outside. The troops in chariots then rode over to the circle formed by Gilgamesh's main force. They positioned themselves facing outward to repel any Assyrians who were thinking of trying to penetrate the inner circle.

Though still great in number, slowly the Assyrians in the circle began to put down their weapons and surrender, knowing it was a battle they could not win in the end. Gilgamesh and Shullat rode their horses to the center of the circle, where the apparent leader of the uprising was standing. He still held his sword in his hand defiantly.

"I will never surrender to you!" he proclaimed to the King. Gilgamesh couldn't help but smirk.

"You won't have to," he replied calmly. Jumping down from his horse, Gilgamesh drew his golden sword from its sheath and stood in front of his opponent. Shullat stood aside amusedly watching. He already knew the outcome.

The leader of the Assyrians lunged at Gilgamesh, who easily parried the sword aside. Again the Assyrian swung at Gilgamesh, missing badly. Gilgamesh seemed to be playing with his opponent as he dodged the lunge of his opponent's sword over and over again effortlessly. Finally, after Gilgamesh had become bored and had enough, he waited for the Assyrian leader to lunge on more time, before slashing his golden sword with inhuman precision and quickness. The Assyrian's lifeless body fell to the ground, his head falling a few feet beside it. Shullat grinned from ear to ear. He loved war! The rest of the Assyrian fighters put their hands up and conceded in fear. Gilgamesh's soldiers rounded them up as he and Shullat rode back to Uruk where most of them would be imprisoned for life or put to work as slaves, while a few of them would be tortured to gather information about any possible Egyptian help they had received. Gilgamesh would want to know of any connection in his future dealing with the Pharaoh.

In the past, before the start of the Egyptian civil war between Northern and Southern Egypt, there had been very friendly relations between the Sumerians and Egyptians. However, when Gilgamesh rose to power, he had isolated his people from them. But Gilgamesh knew that trade between the two empires was to both of their benefit, so he had begun to trade with them again. That is, until Khasekemwy had recently become the new Pharaoh. Near the end of Seth-Peribsen's reign, there were several disputes in his country over which God to follow. The Egyptians had a completely different belief system about who the Gods were than the Sumerians, and there was a great deal of infighting about which God was superior; Horus, the God of the Sky, or Set, the God of the desert. This infighting made the Egyptian empire weak and vulnerable, and Khasekemwy, being one of the Pharaoh's top generals, was able to easily defeat Seth-Peribsen in a military coup. Since then, Khasekemwy had also strained relations with Gilgamesh.

In many ways, they were very similar. While Seth-Peribsen was pragmatic and calm, Khasekemwy was arrogant and ruled Egypt with a mighty fist. He believed that power came at the point of a sword, and had built up the Egyptian military to its largest size and power ever seen. He had also commissioned the building of many temples and stone structures, eager to make his mark on Egyptian history. Much like Gilgamesh who had commissioned the building of the great wall surrounding Uruk, these stone structures were grander than anything built before in Egypt. Gilgamesh had the feeling that war was inevitable with the new Pharaoh, which is why he had Shullat strengthen his own army in size and strength, and outfitted with the unique weapons designed by Dagon.

"I'll bet those dirty Egyptians are behind this!" Shullat exclaimed as Gilgamesh mounted his horse to return to Uruk. "Khasekemwy has been inciting those stupid Assyrians to rise up against us for a long time! And they were stupid enough to believe they could defeat us, just because they gave them badly made Egyptian weapons and supplies. What fools!"

Gilgamesh simply nodded his head and gave his horse a good kick in the side to get going. Shullat followed, all the while still huffing and puffing.

"The Egyptians should pay for this My Lord!" he angrily said. "We should not let them think they can push us!"

"Calm down," Gilgamesh said to Shullat. Shullat grunted, still filled with rage.

"How can you be so calm after those dirty Assyrians tried to overthrow you?!" Shullat asked, quite irritated by his casualness. "I mean, *you*. They tried to overthrow *you*; Gilgamesh! How absurd!!"

"It is nothing to be riled up about my friend," Gilgamesh responded. "There will always be challenges to authority and power. It is the way of the world and as inevitable as the sunrise and sunset. Even people rail against the will of the Gods, which is as hopeless and futile as crossing the Nile River by floating on a rock. We did what we needed to do. Now I want to rest and get back to the business of running my Kingdom."

"I guess you are right My Lord," Shullat said, shaking his head, still obviously frustrated. "But if I were the King," he added, "I would attack Egypt right now, and leave no man, woman, or child alive for this insult!"

"That is why I am King and you are not," Gilgamesh pointedly said. "Being King isn't always about power, my friend. To be pragmatic, you must also rule with your mind."

"Prag...what?" Shullat said, scrunching his face. "My Lord, you know I don't understand such words. And since when have you become such a diplomat? Before your mother died, you ruled your people with the tightest grip of fear I ever knew! And if you ask me, it was much better that way!"

"Things change my friend," Gilgamesh said solemnly as he rode along. "I think when my mother died, I finally understood that."

"I hate change!" Shullat huffed. The two rode in silence for a moment, until Shullat interrupted the silence as a grin formed on his face. "My Lord, don't forget that one of your subjects is getting married tomorrow evening, by the light of the full moon. That should be just the thing to cheer you up!"

Gilgamesh cracked a smile when Shullat informed him of that. He had completely forgotten. Nergal, who had a small shop in the city that made and sold bread, was getting married to Ishara, daughter of the blacksmith Utu. Utu was named after the Sun God Utu, and all of his life, many people had given him a bad time for bearing that name. He had refused to change it though. It was traditional under Gilgamesh's rule, that the King should be able to consort with the wife of any newlywed before the groom. It was his right under the law; and it was just the thing he needed to relax and enjoy himself. Surely he would not please Siduri with this, but it was his right after all, and Ishara was quite beautiful!

Siduri had taken over running his brothel and many of the duties of the Palace since Shamhat had disappeared, and as much as he enjoyed her company and had come to really trust in her, he had come to find out she, in many ways, was even more jealous than Shamhat! Siduri often talked of wanting to become his Queen these last days. But she had begun to gain a little weight, and seemed to become very moody lately. In these days, Gilgamesh had found her less appealing than he had in the beginning. Still, she was much less deceitful and more trustworthy than Shamhat was, and if there ever was someone he would consider taking as Queen, it might be her.

"Go on ahead," Gilgamesh told Shullat. "I am going to ride about for awhile." Shullat shook his head and sighed, then nodded and took off into the distance to return to the Palace. Gilgamesh had become quite introspective lately, and Shullat didn't like it. He thought it showed the kind of weakness that could lead to his destruction by the Egyptians; or anyone else for that matter. Also, it would do little to stop uprisings by the Assyrians and others if they felt the King was weakening.

His concern was genuine. He had been loyal to Gilgamesh, despite his many detractors in the Kingdom who felt he was too cruel and iron-fisted to rule for long. From the beginning of his reign, Shullat had been by his side, having been hand chosen by Gilgamesh to lead his armies. Though Shullat had been a General in Dumuzi's army, he had never really believed in his abilities as a ruler. He saw weakness in Dumuzi, and was proven right when Gilgamesh easily came into Uruk and defeated him. Before that, Shullat had seriously considered a coup of his own to oust Dumuzi. In fact, many of the Generals had. Dumuzi had weakened the strength and image of the mighty Sumerian army, and also their influence over all of the land. It was only when Gilgamesh came to power that the Egyptians and Assyrians once again feared the very mention of their name!

Shullat himself was an Egyptian. His father had fled Egypt during the reign of Pharaoh Senedj, who was the fifth Pharaoh of the Second dynasty of Egypt. Shullat's father had himself been a military leader for Pharaoh Senedj, but fled when Seth-Peribsen came to power. Seth-Peribsen didn't like the cocky, arrogant attitude of his inherited military leader, and ordered him to be executed after he insulted the Pharaoh to his face by calling him a coward, and a "pet" of the Sumerians. Shullat and his father escaped and fled to Kish, where he grew up farming just outside the city. His father trained him intensely in all of the facets of war: how to fight, how to use and fashion weapons, and battle strategy. By the time he was a teenager, Shullat had become exceptionally skilled in all of these areas, and had grown as strong as an ox. He often plowed the field himself without the help of an animal just to strengthen his body.

Shortly after Shullat turned 18, his father died suddenly, and Shullat journeyed into the city of Uruk. He earned his way by performing menial tasks for shopkeepers, often ones that involved great physical strength, as the shopkeepers quickly realized how strong he was. Then, one night, after a bit too much to drink, Shullat had found himself surrounded by some of Dumuzi's guards when he had stumbled onto the Palace grounds. Though they were three, and he was but one, he quickly defeated all of them, killing one, and knocking cold the other two. He was arrested after several more guards heard the commotion and surrounded him. Shullat only spent a few days in the royal prison, before he was summoned to appear before Dumuzi, who had learned of the fight. Dumuzi recognized his talents, and quickly appointed him to be in his army, and from there, Shullat quickly earned his way into becoming one of the Elite guards for Dumuzi. Then he was promoted again to the post of General, where he oversaw many victorious battles against the Assyrians. Though he enjoyed these battles very much, what Shullat really desired was for the Sumerian army to take on the army of the Egyptians. Defeat of the Egyptians would mean total control and domination of all the land, though he had to admit, some of it was personal for him! But Dumuzi had a long-standing treaty with Seth-Peribsen, and was too passive. It was because of this that he quickly changed his allegiance to that of Gilgamesh when he arrived to dethrone Dumuzi.

Gilgamesh rode along in silence by himself, looking out in the sky. It was becoming dark. Another beautiful sunset, he thought to himself. Off in the distance, he could see something. He wasn't sure what it was, but it was bright, and it had captured his attention. It seemed to be some sort of light, or something. But it didn't look like anything he had seen before. It lit up the whole sky over a small area, far to the north. He got a sudden chill in the depth of his soul. Something was coming.

--------------------------------------------------------------------------

Siduri paced back and forth in the house. She had gone home for a few days to see her father. There was something urgent she had felt the need to tell him. But she was terrified to do so! Already she could hear in her head the reaction from her father when he heard the news. He would be furious! But she had put it off as long as she could. Soon, everyone would know anyway. It would be obvious.

Dagon had tolerated his daughter going to be Gilgamesh's closest servant only because he knew that, despite Gilgamesh's arrogance and cruelty, he was intensely fond of Siduri, and would treat her as a princess while in the Palace. His intense hatred of the King, however, was still lingering in his heart. Dagon had watched many friends tortured and executed at the hands of Gilgamesh's army, and Gilgamesh himself. He often took great joy in watching and administering the torture to his rivals. He would cut off various body parts and pour salt in the wounds. He would tie down captives near ant hills, cut them open, and pour honey in the wounds so the ants would infest their bodies. He would drown them in the river until near death, before pulling them back, letting them recover a moment, then doing it again. It made Dagon sick! Dagon was a man of honor and loyalty; beyond this, he believed that you could rule without it being at the end of a sword. Dumuzi was proof of that, before Gilgamesh brutally took over. And now, even though Uruk was militarily feared by all, it was also hated by the rest of the world for its heavy-handed and cruel tactics, its imperialism, its neglect of any rights for its subjects, and the arrogance of the King.

But nothing made his intense hatred of Gilgamesh more real, than witnessing the death of his own wife at the hands of some of Gilgamesh's troops. For that, he would never forgive Gilgamesh, and even though his daughter loved the King, for who knew what reason, he promised himself that he would never really be loyal to him. In fact, he would take any opportunity to kill Gilgamesh if he ever had the chance!

Dagon opened the door of his home to find Siduri there. He immediately broke into a huge smile and ran over to her, lifting her off the ground with his embrace, and kissing her cheek.

"My dear daughter!" he exclaimed. "It has been a long time since I have seen you." Then he put her down and his expression changed. "Why have you not come to visit your own father? Many nights I have worried about your fate under that cruel beast, and you have not even once come to see me until now!"

"Please father," Siduri began. "I am sorry I have not come sooner, but there are so many duties in the Palace. I haven't had time for anything."

"Then why don't you come home," Dagon told her, taking her hands in his, his anger quickly faded. "You don't have to stay there. Just come home to me. You know, it's awfully lonely here nowadays. I have been busy fashioning many weapons for the King which keeps me busy, but when I come home, there is nobody there for me."

"I know father," Siduri said, kissing his forehead. "But I love being in the palace. And I love being in charge of all the duties I have to do for the King....." Siduri trailed off as she stood up and began pacing the floor again.

"What is it Siduri?" Dagon asked her. "There seems to be something troubling you right now." Siduri stopped pacing, her back to her father. She buried her face in her hands and began to cry. Her father stood up and went over to her. He put his hands on her shoulders. "Tell me what it is."

"I can't do it," she whispered to herself, shaking her head. Dagon turned her around gently and put his arms around her.

"Please Siduri," he said, "Tell me what is wrong?" Siduri broke her father's embrace and sat down. Tears were still streaming down her cheeks. "Is it Gilgamesh? Did he do something to you?" Dagon said, his mood changing to anger. "If he did something to you, I swear I will kill him myself!"

"It's not his fault," she said weakly, sniffling.

"*What* is not his fault?" Dagon inquired, becoming more worried by the moment. Siduri did not answer. She sat and stared off into space, still shaking her head. Dagon came over to her and knelt beside her. "What is not his fault?!" he said slowly and deliberately.

Siduri let out a sigh. "Father…..," she began.

"What is it?"

Siduri shook her head again, and then said quietly, still fighting back more tears, "I'm pregnant."

Dagon stood up. Dazed by the words he had just heard, he stood motionless and silent for several moments. Siduri couldn't hold back any longer, and the tears began to flow again. She buried her head in her knees and wept. Dagon paced the floor as his daughter continued to cry, stunned by the news. Every pass he made by her, he could feel his anger building.

"I can assume it is his?" he asked her, stopping in his tracks, his head turned away from her. Siduri looked up at her father, her eyes swelling because of the tears.

"How could you even ask me that?!" she screamed. "Am I some kind of Whore who sleeps with every man she finds? What kind of person do you think I am?!"

Dagon sighed, and ran his hand over his face in frustration. Then he turned to Siduri and said, "I don't know what to think of you anymore." Siduri looked at him in disbelief. Dagon turned and faced her. "I think you are the kind of foolish girl who fell in love with a monster, the Gods only know why, after he kidnapped you from me for his brothel! Then was stupid enough to continue to sleep with him, of her own will no less, knowing that this could be the consequence! What were you thinking? Not at all I suppose! Now you will be lucky if he does not kill you, me, and your child! Yes, because that is the kind of man your 'beloved' King is you ridiculous little girl!"

Dagon slammed his hand into the wall. Siduri sat and stared at her father. She had never known him to speak to her in this manner. "Thank Anu that your mother isn't alive to witness this shameful act!" Dagon continued. "I didn't raise you to be a harlot, but just look at what you have become. A plaything for that Bastard King! You are no better than any of the other prostitutes in his harem that he plays and toys with until he is bored. The same fate awaits you my daughter. What do you think? You think that you are going to be Queen, or something? That the great and powerful Gilgamesh is going to satisfy himself with one woman? It is laughable at best!"

Siduri couldn't take any more of her father's bellowing. She got up and ran out of Dagon's home. She felt betrayed and scared; she felt sick! Her relationship with her father was over now; that much was obvious. After her mother died, she was all he had, and he had always loved her, praised her and treated her like his most precious treasure. Now he was chastising her with the most vicious tongue she had ever heard, and she couldn't believe her ears! Siduri ran as fast as she could back to the Palace, sobbing all the way. She hadn't even bothered to mount her horse; she just wanted away from Dagon as fast as she could. What was she going to do now? There was no one she could turn to but her father, and now, without him, there was no one else she could tell. As much as she wanted to turn around and forgive him, the sting she had given her this day was beyond forgiveness; ever!

Siduri finally arrived at the main entrance to the Palace. One of the guards asked her if she was all right, and she nodded weakly at him, and then proceeded to her chamber. She sat down on her bed and stared at the floor. A million thoughts were running through her head at that moment.

The truth was, she wasn't entirely surprised at her father's reaction. In a way, she had seen it coming. Ever since she had moved into the palace after Shamhat's departure, she had felt her father slipping farther and farther away from her. Her father hated Gilgamesh with all his heart and soul. He had always blamed him for her mother's death, although Gilgamesh wasn't personally there when it happened. He was off hunting down the scattered supporters of Dumuzi, who were still trying to defeat him, even though Uruk had already fallen. Nonetheless, it was Gilgamesh's troops that had slaughtered her. But still, even though he hated Gilgamesh, she never expected the harshness of his words to pierce her heart so badly. She had hoped he could put his hate aside, just for a moment; long enough to offer her love and support. All he had offered her was shame, lectures, and anger!

The only person in the world she was close to except for Gilgamesh had now abandoned her; and she didn't know what she was going to do. She would have to tell Gilgamesh eventually, and she wasn't sure what his reaction would be. In some ways, her father had spoken the truth. Gilgamesh cared for her, that much she was certain. But she had been uncertain that he would ever settle down with one woman. She desperately loved him, and dreamed of being his Queen someday. As time had gone on, however, she was beginning to lose faith in that dream. Perhaps learning that he would have an heir to the throne would bring Gilgamesh even closer to taking her for his Queen; perhaps not.

Siduri began to wonder if this was exactly the same thing that Shamhat had gone through. She had never felt any pity for her before, but now she began to wonder if Shamhat had come to be with Gilgamesh carrying that same dream in her head; of being Queen, only to never see it come any closer to fruition than she did now. Maybe that's why she was so harsh sometimes. Maybe that's why she left. Who knew? Siduri was sure of one thing though; Things between her and Gilgamesh were about to change drastically. Whether it was for the better, or the worse, she would have to wait and see.

---------------------------------------------------------------------------

Shamhat was excited. She was more than excited, she was ecstatic! They had been living in that God-forsaken place with Adad, for what seemed like an eternity. Now they were finally leaving. Enkidu was finally ready to travel to Uruk, and Shamhat's mouth literally watered at the revenge she would have when Enkidu defeated Gilgamesh in battle!

Adad sat on the floor, cross-legged, and ate the breakfast that Shamhat had prepared for him. He would miss her taking care of him, and the help that Enkidu had offered by doing the heavy farm work. If it wasn't for them, he would have surely died by now, he thought. He had lost everything when his son Agga was killed in Uruk. Agga's mother had already died many years ago. Adad had fled to this remote part of the country to escape Gilgamesh's army long before that, but it had been difficult raising Agga without her. But now his caretakers, and friends, were leaving. In his heart, he hoped as much as Shamhat did, that Enkidu would kill Gilgamesh in battle and take the throne. Perhaps then he would feel some justice for the death of his family so many years ago. Furthermore, he was sure that he could return to Uruk and live in the royal palace with Shamhat and the new King. For so long he had lived in poverty outside the Kingdom and maybe now he would have the chance to return to what his life once was!

"It is time Shamhat," Enkidu told her as he entered the tiny house. Her face beamed with excitement as she nodded in agreement. Enkidu turned to Adad and bowed. "We will forever be in debt to you Adad. You provided us with a home after we left the forest, and I will forever be thankful."

"No," Adad told him, standing to his feet. "It is I who should be thankful. You saved my life. I was delirious for a long time after my son's death, and I would have died if it had not been for your intervention. I owe you my life!" Enkidu smiled and extended his arm. Adad took it, and the two embraced, and kissed each other's cheek. "There is something I wanted to tell you," Adad said, "but alas, I am old after all and have forgotten!" Enkidu laughed. Then he turned toward Shamhat and took her hands in his.

"If it is indeed my destiny to face Gilgamesh and defeat him to bring relief to the people of Uruk, then I am ready," he told Shamhat. Shamhat continued to grin from ear to ear. "And you Adad. I don't know how I will repay you for opening your home to us during this time. Whatever my destiny is, I will come again, and bring you back to Uruk."

Adad smiled and nodded his head. "As sad as I am to see you both go, I wish you the best of journeys and luck in defeating that evil creature!" Adad told them both. After a few more embraces and kisses, Enkidu and Shamhat mounted their horses and slowly rode off into the distance. Adad stood at the foot of his home and waved as they disappeared into the morning sun in the background. If Gilgamesh were defeated and dethroned, he would celebrate like no other day in his life, Adad thought! It would mean that Karma will have finally caught up to the mighty King, and he would have to pay for all of the lives he had ruined; especially his! His family was owed this justice!

Suddenly, Adad remembered what he had wanted to tell them. Furiously he began running after them as fast as his old legs could carry him. They were only a short distance away. He could see them after a moment, their horses still plodding slowly along as they chatted.

"Hey!" Adad yelled after them. They didn't seem to notice. Adad yelled after them again, but he was out of breath. He had to stop, and he dropped to his knees in the sand. Even though he had been nursed back to health by Shamhat and Enkidu, he was still weak and old. Enkidu and Shamhat slowly disappeared into the distance again as they continued to ride. Adad caught his breath for a few moments, then stood up and began to walk back to his home.

He wanted to tell them to look for his brother when they were there. He wasn't even sure he was alive, but one of the other fishermen who was often fishing and trapping in the same place as Adad and his son, had told him about a year ago that there was a man who fit that description living in Uruk. The other fishermen often went to Uruk to try to sell the fish he caught to the townspeople. Sometimes they could; other times they sold nothing. Still, it was worth it because they were paid a great deal for the kind of fish that they caught, as it was rare and only lived in the water near the Zagros Mountains. When they had been talking one day, Adad had mentioned he had a brother and what he looked like and did as a profession, but he had not seen him since Gilgamesh took over. Both of them had served under Dumuzi, when he was King. Both

Adad and his brother had been high ranking in Dumuzi's Kingdom.

Adad had lived in the Palace, but also had a small home just outside of the city, and when he had fled with his son after he had lost his wife, he had left something very valuable with his brother. For many years he had often wondered if what he left behind was still safe. He hoped so. The last time he entered Uruk, he lost a piece of himself. One day he would go back to Uruk again, with or without anyone's help, and this time, he hoped to find what he left behind that day. It was, after all, something that could fill the void; another piece of himself.

Shamhat's and Enkidu's donkeys plodded slowly along as they headed for Uruk. It would take a few days to reach it, but after Adad had become well again, he had led them to the water near the woods Enkidu once occupied, and caught several fish for them to eat. They had taken a few in a leather pouch that Enkidu fashioned while staying there for food during the trip, as well as a couple flasks of water from the river. The sun overhead gave no relief though, as it beat down upon them. Shamhat stopped and took the flask of water. She took a large drink and splashed a bit of it on her face and neck. Enkidu smiled when she did this. He couldn't help it. She was very beautiful, even in the torn clothing she was wearing. Enkidu couldn't help but wonder how beautiful she would look in the royal clothing she had always described wearing before she came to him.

"I'm a little nervous," Enkidu said to Shamhat.

"About what?" she asked.

"That I'm going to look foolish when we arrive in Uruk." he replied.

"Why would you say that my love?"

"It's just that, I haven't been around people.....I mean, not that many people at once. I've only lived with you and Adad. There have been a few shepherds and farmers here and there I have met, and even they thought I acted a little strange, but what will I do when I get to Uruk?"

"Don't worry," Shamhat assured him. "You will be fine." They continued to ride on for a moment, then Shamhat added, "and if they don't like you, so what? You are going to be the next King, so they will have to like you then, won't they?"

"I'm not so sure I will be King," Enkidu told her.

"I am," she answered confidently.

"I know that I have been sent here for a reason, but that reason is still not clear to me yet," Enkidu said to her. "And I don't see how it can be that clear to you either."

"I just know it," she said to him. "The Goddess has never failed me. Every time she gave me a vision, it came true. I have used those visions all my life to lift me up to where I was before I left; the most influential woman in all of Sumeria! The one who always had the King's ear and favor. And when you become King, I will still be that woman, only greater. Because you will be the greatest King in history! I am sure of it!" Enkidu raised an eyebrow.

"Why are you so lustful for power Shamhat?" he asked her. She brought her donkey to an abrupt halt and stared over at him.

"What do you mean? Is it some kind of sin for a person to have the best that they can in their lives?"

"No," he replied. "But there is a difference between wanting what will make your life content, and just wanting." Shamhat narrowed her eyes as she listened.

"What are you saying? Are you trying to say that I am some greedy evil person who only wants power and glory? Who are you to say anything to me, anyway? What do you know of being human? You were just an animal before I found you. I am the one who taught you everything you know about humanity. And let me tell you something; if there is one thing that is always true about being human, is that life is often not fair and balanced like it is in nature. We have to scratch and claw at every little thing we have, and there is nothing wrong with setting your dreams as high as you can imagine! If you don't you will always be nothing!"

"And what are your dreams Shamhat?" Enkidu calmly asked. Shamhat looked away from him and stared at the ground for a moment. Then she lifted her head and looked out at the sky.

"One day I *will* rule all of the land of Sumeria. The people will bow down and worship me like a Goddess," she began. Enkidu cocked his head to one side and raised his eyebrows as he listened. "But I will treat them with dignity and respect. I shall conquer all invaders, ensuring their safety. I will make sure there is plenty to eat for everyone, and that all people have a place to stay; that they are treated fairly and have justice. All the things that Gilgamesh has failed to do in his arrogance!" A tear began to roll down her cheek as she spoke. Enkidu reached over and caught the tear with his finger.

"Why are you crying?" he asked her. Another tear streamed down from her eye.

"I wasn't always so great, you know?" she told him jokingly, trying to cheer herself up and keep from completely breaking down. She hated to look weak in front of others. Enkidu chuckled at her attempted joke. "It's true," she continued. "Most of my life I lived poor as a mouse. My father abandoned me when I was a child and I had to live on the street. I had to steal and beg for food just to keep from starving. When I got a little older, I slept with whatever man would give me a bed and something to eat. When there was no man around, I almost froze to death in the cold of the nights because I had nowhere to stay.....You can't even imagine what it's like to have nothing; to do things that are shameful and disgusting, just to try to survive." Shamhat paused a moment as she began to choke up with tears. Enkidu rode his donkey close to hers and put his hand on her shoulder.

"I'm sorry about what your father did to you," he said, trying to console her. Shamhat took a deep breath and wiped away a tear from her eye.

"It's okay," she said half-heartedly. "Anyway, he wasn't my real father to begin with." Enkidu was surprised by this twist in her story.

"He wasn't your real father? What do you mean?"

"Just before he abandoned me," Shamhat started, before pausing a moment to clear the lump in her throat. "He told me I wasn't his daughter….. Of course, I refused to believe it at first. I mean, who would, right? It sounds crazy, but then…..the look in his eyes; after I saw that look…..Well, I knew he was telling the truth."

Enkidu took Shamhat's hand in his and listened on. "He told me that he had found me. Found me in a badly burned down home, just outside of Uruk. He had been passing by, looking for other survivors. All of the homes outside of the city walls had been burnt down, and their occupants slaughtered like cattle; by order of Gilgamesh, of course. Anyway, he had come upon one of the houses and found me still alive. I don't remember it, I was maybe two or three, but he said that despite the fires, I had suffered only a few burns. One is here, on my thigh."

She lifted up her tattered robe and revealed a discolored piece of skin on her upper thigh, about 3 inches in diameter. Enkidu stared at it. He had noticed it before, but had always assumed it was some sort of birthmark or something. He never imagined it had come from a burn.

Shamhat put down her robe again, and continued with her story.

"Anyway, the other is on my head, but you can't see it anymore because my hair has grown over it. But sometimes, when I am outside for a long time in the Sun, and my head gets hot, it begins to burn a little."

"That's terrible," Enkidu told her with sympathy in his eyes.

"It's okay," Shamhat said.

"So he found you there alone?" Enkidu asked.

"No," she told him, "there were two other people there; but they were both dead; a woman and a man, both of them young. They must have been my mother and father, but they had been burned all over their bodies, and the woman had a wound in her chest…..like….like somebody ran her through with a sword or spear"

"No one else?" Enkidu inquired.

"No," she said, shaking her head and sniffling. "At least, that's what he told me. Who knows? Anyway, he took me in and raised me as his daughter. His own wife had been one of the people mindlessly killed by some of Gilgamesh's army as well, and he was about to flee into an outer city and take refuge. He had been looking for other survivors when he found me, and he was kind enough to take me along."

"Why did he tell you all of this," Enkidu asked her.

"I don't know. Maybe he just wanted to hurt my feelings even more. I was a crazy girl, and I did bring him a lot of trouble. That's why he abandoned me I guess," Shamhat said, still sniffling.

"It's still no way to treat someone," Enkidu told her. "He should not have abandoned you!"

"It's okay, I'm over it. Really I am," she assured him. "And anyway, the Gods have a way of making things okay. I did have to suffer for years after that to survive, but just look where I ended up? I was in the Royal Palace, dining on the best food and supervising many servants. And now, I will have the chance to be consort to the greatest King ever!" Shamhat finally broke into a smile when she began to imagine what was ahead. Enkidu broke into a small smirk of his own and shook his head.

"Anyway my love, whenever I see people suffer like I did, it breaks my heart and spirit. I want for no one to endure what I did. But yet, I saw it every day when I was with Gilgamesh. They way he treated his subjects; let people starve outside the walls of the city; killed or imprisoned people at his whim for no reason; tortured the captured soldiers of other armies. I know that the people have been praying for some relief from the Gods; for them to send someone who could challenge and defeat him so they could have peace in their lives again. That someone is you Enkidu! When you defeat Gilgamesh, I will be right there by your side, guiding you in the politics of the land. You have no experience in such things, but I can be your most precious advisor of all; I can be your Queen, and together we can bring justice and peace to all Sumeria!"

Enkidu sat and listened to her entire reasoning, and though it was very convincing, he was a still just a little concerned in his heart about her true motives. But in his heart he also knew that she was right in one sense; his destiny was waiting for him in Uruk. He was drawn to that place by an unseen force in the deepest part of his soul. It was as if a part of him would not be complete until he went there. He couldn't explain the feeling, but it must have been put there by the Gods. So he would continue to follow her for now. He needed her after all. He knew nothing of human culture except what she had taught him, and he needed her to guide him in Uruk and help him fit in with other humans. And should it be his destiny to face Gilgamesh, and defeat him as she said, then he would have to decide in his own heart whether to trust her judgment or not.

The sun was beginning to set on them as they traveled. They decided to stop and lay on a straw mat they had taken from Adad's home and rest. As they lay there, a brilliant flash of light was showing in the sky above them. It was beautiful. Enkidu looked over at Shamhat, but she had immediately fallen asleep in her exhaustion from the trip. Enkidu wasn't tired at all. Though tamed by Shamhat a bit, he still possessed the stamina of the animals. The light hung over the two of them high in the sky. He wasn't sure what the light was, but he was sure it was sent from above. The Gods must be watching over him, he told himself. At least, someone must be.

---------------------------------------------------------------

"Well what did you think would happen?" Shullat told her as she sat on her bed and explained what had happened with her father. Siduri's eyes were still red from crying, and she was both physically and mentally exhausted. Shullat had been walking by her room when he heard her crying, and came in to see if she was all right.

"I thought that he's my father, and that he would have some kind of understanding," she told Shullat. "I'm his only daughter, and he treated me like some piece of trash to be thrown away when you don't want it anymore!" Shullat nodded his head. In actuality, Shullat could care less if Siduri was fine. He had been very upset when Shamhat had disappeared and Siduri had taken her place these last few months. Shamhat and Shullat had grown quite close during her years there, and though Shullat was a loner, he had taken a fancy to Shamhat and her razor sharp wit. It also didn't hurt that she was beautiful as well! He often had fantasized about her in that way, but Shamhat always had her eyes fixed on the King.

But since Gilgamesh was infatuated with Siduri now, he thought it wise to get to know her. In some ways, Siduri reminded him a bit of Shamhat; from a distance, one could even mistake one for the other, a fact that Aruru had mentioned to him before she, herself, had disappeared right after Shamhat. He hadn't seen her since either; not that he was complaining.

"It's not something I wouldn't expect from Dagon!" he said to Siduri. "You know that I knew your father when he was still making weapons for King Dumuzi. Even then he was insufferable! Dumuzi wanted to make him a General in his army, because he was very intelligent, and could make the finest weapon and shield designs in all Sumeria."

"I didn't know any of that," Siduri said with a perplexed look on her face. "He never told me that he was offered to be a General."

"It's true. It was his short temper and stubbornness that kept him from being a General. In fact, Gilgamesh initially wanted him killed when he seized power, and asked *me* to take care of it." Shullat paused a moment to stroke his beard that he had been growing out recently these past few months. "But even though I didn't really like your father that much, nor do I now for that matter, I knew that he was the best. *I was the one* who persuaded Gilgamesh to keep him alive and keep forging weapons and armor for his army. It's a matter of fact that because of me, your father and you are still alive!"

"I had no idea," Siduri said, amazed at what she was hearing. "I had no idea about any of it." She had known nothing of these things. She knew that her father hated Gilgamesh, but she didn't know that he had forged weapons for Dumuzi, nor been offered to be a General in his army. She always thought he had started to design weapons for Gilgamesh only. Dagon had not wanted to discuss anything about the past with her, even though she had asked on many occasions. He said it was too painful to think about and it was best she didn't know.

"In fact," Shullat continued, being quite amused that he was spilling the beans about many things her father had not told her, "he had a brother who worked in the palace for Dumuzi as well." Siduri looked at Shullat a moment, her mouth dropped open.

"What?" she finally said, almost inaudibly. She was stunned at the news.

"That's right. I can't remember his name, but he was close to Dumuzi, this I know. He was his most trusted advisor. When Gilgamesh took over, he fled Uruk. Nobody has seen him since. Anyway, if I did see him, I would probably kill him!"

"I can't believe it!" Siduri exclaimed. "I have an Uncle! And I didn't even know about it!"

Shullat chuckled. "Anyway, the point is that your father is who he is. And *you* are someone that Gilgamesh likes very much. That in itself is worth more than anything your father could ever do for you. You don't need your father anymore; in fact, you don't really need anyone. You have the ear of the most powerful ruler of all time; that is all you need!"

"Maybe you are right Shullat," Siduri said, nodding her head in agreement. Why *did* she need her father anyway? She loved him very much because he was her father, but what he did to her she would never forget! Maybe forgive, but never forget! And Shullat was right; she had the ear of the King. It was one step from being his Queen. She had everything she needed right there, in the Palace. "Thank you for listening to me Shullat. I appreciate it, really."

"It's quite alright child," he told her, putting his hand on her shoulder. "And I won't tell anyone about your situation." Siduri smiled. Shullat smiled back, then took his hand away and began to leave.

"You're not going already, are you?" Siduri asked Shullat, batting her eyelashes. Shullat turned back toward Siduri, who was giving him the look of a puppy, who's master was about to leave.

"I must get down to inspect the armory," Shullat told her matter-of-factly. Siduri continued to look at him with her eyes wide and lashes batting. He was starting to feel a little uncomfortable with how Siduri was looking at him. The last thing he needed was trouble from the King!

"I can come with you," Siduri told him, stepping forward and putting her hand on his arm. "That is, if you want me to." Shullat could smell her sweet scent as she came close to him and the baby soft skin of her fingers on his arm. He couldn't deny that she was very beautiful, and he was very tempted in this moment. He could feel his heart begin to pump a bit faster. Siduri smiled and ran her fingers along his arm as she waited for his answer.

"I....Uh....I...well.....I..." Shullat was stumbling for words as he tried to move subtly away from Siduri, but she matched every step and stayed close.

"Don't you want me to keep you company Shullat?" she cooed in his ear. "It must be very lonely to be down in the armory all by yourself at this hour." Siduri blew into Shullat's ear as she spoke, and he could feel his cheeks turning red and his heart racing. She was becoming incredibly persuasive. Shullat had not been tempted by anyone so much, except for Shamhat. He was beginning to realize her appeal to Gilgamesh. He was about to give in and invite her with him, when he was suddenly interrupted by a loud crash. It was the door to Siduri's chamber being swung open and hitting the wall behind it. Standing there in the doorway was the King.

"My Lord!" Shullat exclaimed loudly, moving abruptly away from Siduri. "You have returned." Gilgamesh stood and stared at the two of them from across the room, and then he slowly began to walk over to them.

"What is going on here?" he asked the two of them. Shullat looked over at Siduri, who had her head down, looking at the floor.

"Nothing my love," Siduri softly replied, not looking at him. Gilgamesh stopped and looked at Siduri for a

161

moment. Then his eyes shifted over to Shullat. Immediately, Shullat looked down, not looking Gilgamesh in the eye. He had done nothing wrong yet, but he dare not risk the wrath of the King if he had gotten the wrong idea about what was going on between them.

"Are you not supposed to be inspecting the armory right now Shullat?" Gilgamesh asked him. Shullat nodded quickly, then bowed to the King and scuffled out the door of Siduri's chambers. Siduri was still frozen in her spot, not looking at Gilgamesh.

"Why do you not look at me Siduri?" he asked her.

"I.....I just thought.....maybe...."

"Maybe what?" he asked.

"That perhaps you had gotten the wrong impression my Lord," she whispered, still looking down at the floor. Gilgamesh cocked his head to one side, and then let out a sigh.

"And what do you think I would get the wrong *impression* about?" Gilgamesh asked somewhat mockingly. Siduri shrugged her shoulders, but didn't answer. Gilgamesh walked slowly over to her, and circled around her a few times, all the while keeping his eyes fixed on her. She glanced up a few times to see what he was doing, but only for a moment. Her face was beet red. She was embarrassed by what he had seen and heard. Suddenly Gilgamesh stopped in front of her. Gently he put his hand up to her chin and raised her head slowly until their eyes met. Gilgamesh smiled at her, and Siduri weakly smiled back. For a moment, she thought everything was all right. That's the last thing she remembered.

She woke up to the sunlight blaring in her face. It felt as though she had been sleeping for days. Her head hurt, and her neck and back were sore. She tried to get up, but it was too painful. The room seemed to be spinning. Everything around her was blurry, and she felt as though she might vomit. Siduri quickly closed her eyes and lied back on the pillow. Her jaw ached with a dull and constant pain. She wasn't sure where she was. She assumed that it was her chambers, but she couldn't make out anything. Something stirred next to her suddenly, and she called out.

"Who is it?" she asked as strongly as she could. Her voice was as quiet as a mouse in reality though, for she had no strength. She felt a hand on her shoulder, patting it gently. Then she heard a voice. It was a familiar one.

"How are you feeling Siduri?" the voice asked. It was a woman's voice. She knew it well. Her name was Delondra. She had been with Gilgamesh for almost three years, since she just turned 15. The time was soon coming that she would reach her 18th birthday, and be allowed to leave. She had medium length coal black hair and soft brown eyes. She was quite tall and wiry also. When she stood next to Gilgamesh, the top of her head came to his chin, which was unusual for any woman. She was one of the concubines in the harem, the only one actually, who liked Siduri. Most of them were quite jealous of her rise to favor and power so swiftly. Some of the concubines had been with Gilgamesh for a great deal longer than Siduri, but they had been condemned to stay in the harem and pleasure him at a moment's notice.

Even though he had been with Siduri quite often these past few months, he still requested one of his concubines at least twice a week. It had been a double-edged sword for Siduri, who loved being the top woman in the Palace. One of her duties was to keep watch over the harem, and personally bring the concubine of Gilgamesh's choice to his chamber when he requested it. Sometimes Siduri could feel her blood boil with jealousy when she had to perform this task, but she did it, nonetheless.

Siduri tried to sit up again, but Delondra put her hand on her chest and gently forced her back down. "You must not try to get up right now," she told her. "You almost died you know."

"What?" was all Siduri could weakly muster. Things were still a bit hazy. She remembered talking to Shullat about her father. But then what happened? She couldn't remember. Delondra began to hum as she stroked Siduri's hair. She had always been envious of it. It was so long and smooth. Delondra's hair was long, but frizzy. No matter what she did to try to tame it, it wildly and defiantly stuck up in the air in all directions. She even once tried cutting it, a social taboo, just to see if it would be easier to manage, but it only made it wilder. Whatever Delondra was humming was beginning to annoy Siduri, and she tried to get up from the bed again. This time, Delondra pushed her down with a bit more force.

"Hey!" Siduri cried out. Delondra bowed her head and smiled.

"Forgive me Siduri, but it is by the order of the King that you remain in bed for the rest of the week," Delondra told her.

"What? The order of the King you say?" Siduri said incredulously. She began to sit up again, but once again was forced down by Delondra. Even when Siduri was healthy she could not fight with Delondra; she was just too tall and strong.

"That is right Siduri," said Delondra. "Gilgamesh wants to make sure you are fully healthy again before you resume your duties." Siduri gave up, and lied back down on the bed. Suddenly, she had a moment of clarity; Gilgamesh! When Delondra had said that name, it broke something loose in her head. She started to remember what she was doing there in the first place. She had been talking to Shullat when Gilgamesh had interrupted them. Shullat left, and then.....what happened? She remembered that Gilgamesh had been very angry about something. Was it the Egyptians....or Shamhat....or Shullat; what was it? And what happened to her? Had she fallen down or something? The pain in her jaw began to intensify. It became a shooting pain. She could feel her heartbeat as the pain reached her temple. It was agonizing! Delondra put her hand on Siduri's forehead.

"Are you okay?" she asked her. Siduri put her hands on the sides of her head. It felt as though her head was about to split. Her breaths were coming long and deep as she tried to fight the pain.

"That wound you have on your chin is beginning to bleed again," Delondra told her. "Do you wish me to fetch the Asu?" Siduri nodded her head weakly. Delondra got up from the side of the bed and scurried off to find Puzur, the head Asu of the Palace. An Asu was a type of physician. Siduri was sweating intensely, and she felt feverish. Gilgamesh; the only thing stuck in her mind was that name. She desperately tried to remember what he was angry about, but she could barely focus on any thought with the intense pain in her head and jaw. And anyway, whatever he was angry about. He should have been there by her side, shouldn't he? Didn't he supposedly care about her more than any other girl? Gilgamesh; Where was he and what was he doing right now?!

Suddenly a wave of terror came over her. The baby; She had been so confused and dazed by the whole situation, she had forgotten she was pregnant for a moment! Siduri put her hand on her stomach. She was still very early in her pregnancy, so she still could not feel a thing; nor did she physically show yet that she was with child. She didn't feel any pain in her stomach. That was a good sign. It was probably the only place that she didn't feel pain though. Sighing in relief, she let her hand drop back down to her side and closed her eyes. Just then, Delondra came back in the room.

"I couldn't find the Asu Siduri," she informed her. "He must be in town to celebrate with everyone else."

"Celebrate what?" Siduri asked her rather confused. Delondra just smiled and stroked her hair again.

"Don't you remember Siduri? This is the day of the wedding." Siduri looked at Delondra with a befuddled look on her face. "You know, the wedding between Nergal and Ishara."

"Nergal? Ishara?"

"Don't worry. You had quite the bad day yesterday, didn't you? Anyway, I wouldn't expect that you would be anything less than hazy," Delondra said. She got up from Siduri's side and stood over her. "By the way," she began, "how far along are you?" Siduri's eyes grew wide.

"What do you mean?" she asked Delondra, trying to play dumb.

"I mean how long have you been pregnant?" Delondra said, shaking her head and playfully smiling. Siduri was speechless. She sat with her mouth wide open, not knowing exactly what to say. Delondra finally broke the silence.

"It's okay Siduri. You don't have to tell me if you don't want to. And I won't say anything to anyone."

"But.....but how did you know?" Siduri asked her.

"I just know things," she replied. "Sometimes I can just look at someone and images will flash in my head; things about them now, or in the past, or even sometimes the future. I've always been able to do it since I was very little."

"Why didn't you ever tell me?" Siduri inquired. Delondra smiled and shook her head.

"I've only told a few people in my life," she said. "And they all thought I was either crazy or possessed by an evil spirit or something." Delondra began to stroke Siduri's hair again while she spoke. Siduri lied in her bed and listened intently. "Even my own mother thought I was possessed! Once, she called an Ashipu over to where we lived; so he could try to "cure" me."

"Really? She brought one of those Sorcerers?" Siduri exclaimed.

"Oh yes. But anyway, there was nothing he could do for me because I wasn't possessed. I just can see things sometimes. Not always, and I don't know when it will happen. But when I found you lying there last night, all alone and bleeding, and hurt, I had a vision of you with a baby in your arms. I don't know why I had this vision at that moment." Siduri looked down at her stomach and put her hand over it.

"You are right Delondra," she told her, with a timid voice, "I am pregnant."

"I know," she replied, grinning. She picked up the clay cup that was sitting beside Siduri. "I'm going to fetch you some more water."

"Thank you," Siduri said to her. Delondra smiled and began to leave the room. She stopped and looked back at Siduri.

"You know, I could fetch you *another* drink," she told her. Siduri looked confused. Delondra came back over to her bed and sat down on the end of it. "You're not the only one you know. There have been many other times that concubines have learned they were pregnant by the King. When Aruru was here, Gilgamesh would order the girl to go to her. She would whip up a "special" drink to make them all better." Siduri shifted her eyes away from Delondra, trying to take in what she way saying. "Anyway, she's disappeared with Shamhat, but I'm sure that I can remember what she put in it; sometimes she let me help her mix it; that is, if you want me to?" Siduri thought for a moment, and then looked up at Delondra.

"No," she told her definitively. Delondra bowed her head, and then proceeded to leave to fetch the water. It almost looked like she was floating every time she walked. It was so quiet that if you were to close your eyes, you couldn't tell that anyone was walking at all. Siduri wasn't sure what to think. In a way, she was relieved that someone else knew about it except for her father; but on the other hand, what if she told everyone in the Palace? She would be shunned and mocked; and what about

Gilgamesh? She hadn't even had the chance to tell him about it before what happened with Shullat......

"Wait a minute," Siduri said aloud to an empty room. Her heart began to race and her breaths became short. She suddenly began to recall what had happened. Tears began to roll down her cheeks as she remembered the horrible event.

She put her hand up to her face and began to weep. How could he do that to her? How could he?! It was all clear to her again. She shuddered as the harsh images replayed in her head. Still crying uncontrollably, Siduri lied back down on the bed. How could he do that to her? Someone he said he loved? Why?! If her baby died, she would never forgive him. That was for sure!

It was at that moment that she decided she would never tell Gilgamesh she was pregnant. Her father had been right about him all along. He would probably kill her and the baby if he found out. She was sure he was capable of anything now! Siduri called out for Delondra, who appeared in the doorway a moment later. She would have to make sure that Delondra didn't tell Gilgamesh either. Siduri had to convince her any way she could or it might be a death sentence for both of them!

Enkidu stood in the hot sand, his donkey by his side, and peered out into the distance. Shamhat was sitting and fanning herself with her hand, trying to cool down, but it was impossible. The sun had only begun to rise, but it was already unbearably hot. The top of her head was beginning to burn in the sun. This was one of the hottest times of the year in fact, and there they were, trying to cross the desert to get to the boundaries of Uruk, she thought to herself! She opened up the top of a small clay flask where they had taken water with them to drink, but found nothing but mocking emptiness. She was so thirsty! Enkidu finally came over to Shamhat and sat down beside her.

"I can see the great wall that you described," Enkidu proudly told her. Shamhat looked at him for a moment, not quite believing what he said.

"How can you see it? It must be at least five or ten miles away still!" she said.

"No, only about two or so," he replied. "I can tell."

"What? What do you mean? Are you trying to tell me that you can see the wall from two miles away? That's impossible!" Shamhat chuckled.

"You do not believe me?" Enkidu asked. Shamhat continued to smirk, and shook her head. "You have seen me perform many feats any ordinary man could not possibly do, but you doubt this?"

"You are incredibly fast and strong my love," she said, putting her hand on his shoulder and rubbing it, "but to see two miles away? That's impossible, even for Gilgamesh; and he is part God himself!' Enkidu raised an eyebrow, and then thought for a moment.

"Alright," he began, standing to his feet, "I will tell you something that I could not possibly know about the wall unless I have seen it. Just tell me what you want me to tell you about it."

Shamhat stood to her feet. "Alright then," she said, pacing around in a circle, trying to think of something he would only know if he had witnessed it. She finally stopped and faced Enkidu. "Tell me about the guards at the wall."

"What do you want to know," he asked her.

"Everything," she replied, still smirking. "What they are wearing; the color of their hair; where they are standing….."

"Very well," Enkidu told her, and then he turned to the direction of Uruk. He peered out into the distance for a moment, his eyes turning a glowing light yellow color. All the while, Shamhat smiled and laughed at him under her breath.

"Is it too hard? Shall I give you something easier?" she said, teasing him.

"Not at all," Enkidu said, turning back to where she was standing. Shamhat almost jumped when she saw his yellow eyes, but they soon faded back into his normal brown color. "There are two men. One is tall; about 6 feet, and he is holding a spear in his left hand, and a golden shied in his right." Shamhat's smile disappeared. "The other is shorter, about 5 ½ feet or so," he continued, "and his hair is grey; he is older. He is carrying a sword in his right hand and a shield in his left. They are both wearing Golden armor on their chest, and have some sort of axe at their sides, though I've never quite seen a design such as this from any trapper or farmer I have met."

"That is amazing!" Shamhat exclaimed. He had been exactly right. The two guards outside of the wall were exactly as he had described. The tall one, Atra, always carried his shield in his right hand, while Dingu, the older guard, always carried his shield on the opposite arm. Shamhat had often wondered why they carried it on opposite arms, but had never really cared enough to ask them. Also, they always wore their socket axes around their waists, and had golden plated armor on their torsos. Shamhat was thoroughly impressed. Not even Gilgamesh could do such a thing!

"We should be able to reach the wall in just a few hours now; by early evening." Enkidu told her. Shamhat nodded her head, and lied down on a small mat she had been sitting on to keep from burning her skin. The sand was fiery hot, and the breeze of wind that blew by them felt as though they were standing next to fire. Enkidu still had most of his water left in his flask, and he offered it to

Shamhat. He felt bad for her. Ordinary humans would quickly die without water, but not him. In the forest, he had often gone weeks without water when he had to; kind of like a camel, he supposed. It was ingenious how the Gods had made his abilities like those of the animals that surrounded him. It had allowed him to blend in with nature and live among them, and allowed him to survive in the harshest of conditions.

"Thank you," Shamhat said to Enkidu, gulping down the water he had given her. "How is it that we have traveled all this way and your flask was still almost full? Don't you need to drink?"

"You saw me drink all the time," he told her, smiling. "But, I knew that you would run out of water quickly, so I saved mine for you." Shamhat blushed and looked away. She was flattered he had been thinking of her before himself. She wasn't sure that any man before had done that. All of them wanted something from her when they were nice and accommodating. "Anyway, don't worry. I can go for many days, even weeks without drinking."

"You never cease to amaze me," she said, blowing him a kiss. Enkidu smiled as he pretended to catch it. Shamhat stood up and took the mat from the sand. She dusted it off, and then packed it back on her donkey. "We need to get going if we are to catch Gilgamesh in the evening. I'm sure he will be out patrolling for another prize girl to have fun with. It will be the perfect opportunity to confront him." Enkidu simply nodded his head and jumped up on his donkey. Shamhat followed suit, and they began to ride off toward the wall.

"Shamhat…" Enkidu began to say. She looked over at him.

"What is it?"

"Well….." he started again before pausing.

"Well what?"

"Well, what will I do if I fight Gilgamesh and become King?" Enkidu asked her.

"What do you mean?" she replied.

"I don't know anything about running a kingdom," he told her nervously.

"That's why you have me my love," she reminded him. Enkidu thought for a moment.

"Why would the Gods have me challenge Gilgamesh if I don't know anything about being a King? For that matter, I barely even know what it's like to live as a human. For so many years I lived as an animal. If I am destined to be the King, then why did the Gods put me in the forest?"

"Who knows such things but the Gods themselves," she said, shrugging her shoulders.

"It just doesn't make sense…..some things. I am not sure about anything sometimes. I mean, sometimes I believe this is my path, but other times I have doubts."

"Believe me Enkidu," she told him, "This is just where you are supposed to be. I am sure of it."

"Why?"

"I just am, that's all," she answered, becoming a bit irritated at his sudden introspection.

"I don't know," he sighed as they rode along. Something out of the corner of his eye caught his attention. He stopped his donkey and looked around. On one side of them were a few trees. He thought he saw one of the trees moving.

"What is it my love," Shamhat asked him, stopping her donkey also. Enkidu put his hand up, calling for quiet, as he looked around some more. He took a deep breath of the air around him. He smelled something. One of the branches of the trees was moving. Something, or someone, was behind one of the trees. He jumped down from his donkey and watched the trees slowly. There was no hint of a breeze anymore, but sure enough, after a moment, one of the trees began to sway a little. Enkidu looked over at Shamhat, who had a concerned look on her face. He smiled and winked at her, then with all his might, jumped from the spot he was standing. Shamhat looked up and saw that he had jumped very high in the air, like he had done in the forest when they had first met. The tree began to sway a lot more, as Enkidu landed right in front of it, about 50 feet away from where he was standing. Out from behind it stumbled a small woman. She tried to run, but Enkidu quickly caught her and flung her over his shoulder. She pounded on his back and cursed at him, trying to get free. Shamhat turned her head and listened to the woman's voice. It was very familiar. Suddenly she realized who it was. That raspy voice was unique. It was Aruru!

"Aruru!" Shamhat yelled, leaving her donkey and running over to where Enkidu was standing. Aruru stopped pounding her fists on Enkidu's back and looked over at Shamhat. Her eyes grew wide and a smile formed on her face. Enkidu looked at Shamhat running over to where he was, and then pointed his finger at Aruru's rear side.

"Is this a friend of yours?" he asked Shamhat, as she came to a stop in front of him.

"Yes," she answered, trying to catch her breath. Enkidu dropped Aruru onto the ground. She landed with a thud.

"Hey!" she shouted at Enkidu. Aruru got to her feet and glared at Enkidu. She put her hands on her hips and stepped up close to him. She only came to just above his stomach, but she stared at him as if she wanted to fight. Shamhat shook her head and grinned. Same old Aruru, she thought to herself. Someday she would wind up getting herself killed because of her temper.

"Aruru, what are you doing out here?" Shamhat asked her old friend. Aruru continued to try to stare down

Enkidu, who was now chuckling to himself at this little girl's courage. He even found it impressive and admirable. Shamhat put her hands on Aruru's shoulders.

"Come one Aruru," she begged her. Aruru slowly allowed Shamhat to pull her away from where she was standing, and they both sat down in the sand a few feet away under one of the trees. Enkidu shook his head and laughed as Aruru continued to glance over with a menacing look on her face. He turned and walked away so the two women could re-acquaint themselves.

"Who is that thing?" Aruru asked in her classically candid approach. Shamhat couldn't help but smile. She had missed Aruru and her straightforward, no-fear attitude.

"That thing is the best thing that could happen to me," she told her.

"What? What the heck are you talking about Shamhat? And where have you been for these past months?"

"I was with Enkidu," Shamhat told her.

"En.....who?" Aruru said confusedly.

"It's a long story Aruru. Anyway, what in the world are you doing all the way out here?"

"I just couldn't stay in the palace another day with that monster," Aruru replied. She balled her hand up into a fist as she spoke. "Ever since you left, guess who has the ear of Gilgamesh now? Siduri, that's who! That little tramp!"

"Siduri?" Shamhat said, her eyes growing wide in disbelief. "Siduri took my place?!"

"That's right Shamhat, and now she is managing all his affairs. The concubines can't stand her though, and many of the servants were very upset when you left.....hey, you didn't answer the question! Where have you been, and where did you find that monkey over there?"

"He's not a monkey," Shamhat said, smiling.

"Well, who is he, and why is *he* the best thing that could happen to you?"

Shamhat took Aruru's hands in hers. "I had a vision Aruru. You know, one of my dreams."

"Really?" Aruru said. "What was it about?"

"It was from Ishtar. I am sure of it, and it was about him. So I went out to the forests to the North with a man named Adad to try to find him."

"Who's Adad?"

"Never mind," Shamhat said. "Anyway, I found him living in the forest and I knew that I had been sent there to retrieve him."

"This is all really weird," Aruru told her with a strange look on her face. "Are you sure you haven't suffered from heat exhaustion or something?"

"No Aruru. Anyway, long story short, this is the man who will be the next King of Sumeria! And I will be his Queen. Finally, I will be Queen!" Shamhat declared, clapping her hands together.

"If you say so Shamhat," Aruru answered without much conviction.

"Don't you believe me?" Shamhat asked.

"I don't know Shamhat; it's a pretty wild story. But then again, I guess about anything is possible anymore. But I'll tell you something. If this man can defeat Gilgamesh and become King, I'm all for it; anything would be better than what we have now. I thought that after his mother died he had become a bit better, but after you disappeared and Siduri has his attention, it seems that maybe he has become even crueler than before!"

"What do you mean?" Shamhat inquired.

"I left about a month ago, but right before I did, I had overheard how Gilgamesh had one of his servants killed because he didn't like the way he looked at him. And I know that he has tortured and killed many of the stragglers outside of the city walls because they supported the Assyrians."

"That's terrible," Shamhat said.

"And one more thing," Aruru said, leaning in closer, "I am sure that Siduri is plotting to become his Queen! She thinks that she is going to rule by Gilgamesh's side! If anyone should be Queen, it should be you Shamhat."

"Oh but I will be," she assured her friend. "I will be; but it won't be with that bastard King we have now. I don't care if he is part God or how powerful he thinks he is. I am sure that *my* champion can defeat him. He can do things I have never seen before Aruru. His power is truly from the Gods! You saw how high and far he jumped to catch you, didn't you?"

"Yes," Aruru admitted, nodding in agreement. "It was amazing. But I have seen Gilgamesh smash through walls with his bare fists. I have seen him uproot trees with his hands, and throw boulders of rock to a target 300 feet away! Are you sure this man can defeat him?"

"I have also witnessed all these things Aruru," Shamhat said to her. "And I have known Gilgamesh much longer than you. I am fully aware of what he can do, and I tell you again, that I know Enkidu can defeat him." Shamhat smiled and put her hands on Aruru's shoulders. "And then I *WILL* be Queen! And you will be right there by my side to share my glory!"

"Thank you Shamhat," Aruru gratefully said, taking her hand. She sighed a hopeful prayer for revenge to be taken on Gilgamesh and Siduri. She didn't care who it was that defeated Gilgamesh, just as long as Gilgamesh and Siduri suffered greatly! That would be the only thing to make her heart happy, she told herself.

"And I know the perfect opportunity," Aruru proudly announced. Shamhat listened intently. "There is a wedding this evening between Nergal and Ishara. Surely you know that Gilgamesh will want to, you know, before Nergal does. It is his law after all!" Shamhat was thrilled at the news, and nodded her head gleefully. Aruru giggled.

"This is even better," Shamhat said. "All of the people of Uruk will be there in Inanna's temple no doubt. Not only will I know where to find Gilgamesh, but all of the townspeople can witness my champion defeat him!"

"It's perfect!" Aruru squealed.

"Speaking of Enkidu, where is he?" Shamhat asked. Aruru shrugged her shoulders and the two of them stood up and began to search around for Enkidu. They didn't realize he had been there the whole time. Enkidu looked down on the two women searching for him from the top of one of the trees they were sitting under. He let out a long sigh as he watched them wander about, calling his name. Enkidu finally knew what he had long suspected. Was he really called to do this? Defeating Gilgamesh would be good for the people of Uruk he supposed, but it also seemed that he would be doing the bidding of these two less than noble women also. It would feed their need for revenge and lust for power. He began to wonder if all humans were like this. Maybe it was just part of their nature, he wondered. In any event, it was too late to turn back now. He had his destiny to fulfill, and despite what he had just heard, he still believed that Uruk was where he was supposed to be. Just a feeling he had. Maybe it would be to fight the King; maybe not. In a few hours he would know for sure.

--------------------------------------------------------------

Gilgamesh rode through the city's main thoroughfare with four guards flanking him on each side. Shullat rode just ahead of him, shouting at townspeople to get out of the way.

"Move it!" Shullat shouted at one man. The man didn't move fast enough for Shullat's liking, so he kicked his horse's side, causing it to buck up in the air. The horse's front hoof hit the man squarely in the head, and he fell to the ground bleeding profusely from his skull. Shullat bellowed in laughter. Gilgamesh simply smirked and looked away. A few of the other townspeople began to pick the man up, but Shullat glared them down until they slithered away, not wanting to suffer the same fate.

About 50 feet away, in front of the procession, was Nergal and Ishara. They had just been married in the temple of Inanna and were now standing just outside the temple entrance. It was the largest of four temples in the great city, and was the only one that had been constructed completely of Limestone, making it unique to the others. The other three temples were devoted to Anu, the Father of the Gods, and the chief God of the city of Uruk. Inanna was the Goddess of love, which is why the wedding took place there.

Ishara was wearing many necklaces and rings made of Gold and Silver; gifts from Nergal, as per the custom, as well as a Nundunnu, which was a special gift given to the bride at the time of marriage. Nergal's father, Utu, had made her a headpiece made entirely of Gold and Gemstones. It was quite a sight to behold, but then again, Utu was one of the finest blacksmith in Uruk after all. In fact, Dagon, after designing many of the weapons and armor for the army, usually requested that Utu assist him in forging some the weapons from the metal he provided in the fire. If Nergal and Ishara ever divorced, the Nundunnu was the only thing that the bride could legally keep.

The ceremony had been relatively simple compared to the long and complicated Assyrian wedding rituals, which often lasted for days. On the other hand, it was more formal than the Egyptians, who, when two people decided they wanted to be married, simply moved in together in the same place. In the temple of Inanna, Nergal and Ishara had stood with a priest and their two families present. The other townspeople had to wait outside until the ceremony was over, but would put on quite the festival to celebrate it once completed. Nergal had put a veil over

Ishara and declared publicly to the priest and the two families, as well as the Gods, that she was his wife. After that he was required to pour perfume over her head, and then deliver the gifts of Gold and Silver to her, as well as the Nundunnu. When this was done, Ishara became a full member of Nergal's family.

Ishara was young and beautiful. Nergal had counted himself lucky to have been able to marry her, as many young suitors had been chasing her. She was short, but not as short as Aruru, and she had a very curvy figure, dark brown eyes, and a beautiful face that made men lust when they saw her. It was this fact that had made Gilgamesh very happy to see her married. Now he could have his way with her without taking her as a concubine, in accordance to the law; his *own* laws albeit. Anyway, Ishara had escaped the clutches of Gilgamesh long enough to now be 19 years old, and too old for the harem. It was an agreement he had with Utu that as long as he served Dagon and him, he would not take Ishara into his brothel. Dagon had been very angry after he had taken Siduri from him, seeing as how he had this long arrangement with Utu.

As Gilgamesh made his way to the temple, he saw the entire area filled with his subjects. It was a time of great celebration when someone was married, but there was trepidation in the air as well. They all knew what was to come, and while most felt it unjust, they dare not say anything or they risked being punished severely.

Peering out from the crowd was Shamhat. She hid herself in the swarm of townspeople and watched

Gilgamesh's every move with vengeance in her eyes. Aruru was on the opposite side of the crowd to Gilgamesh's left. Enkidu stood in the crowd, but made no effort to conceal himself. He still felt a little out of place being surrounded by this mass of people, and he was still unsure as to what he would do when he saw the King. Now Gilgamesh was approaching, and he looked at him as he rode to the entrance of the temple to meet Ishara and Nergal. Gilgamesh's stature was equal to that of his own, something he hadn't noticed among any of the other people he had seen or met. It was almost as if the Gods had made them equal in stature; maybe as a balance.

He watched Gilgamesh intently as he rode. The King was graceful and handsome. Enkidu wished he had been given the grace and looks of the King as well, not just his stature. Gilgamesh looked in the direction where Shamhat was standing, but she quickly ducked behind another woman in the crowd to avoid detection. Just as his horse arrived at the temple, Gilgamesh looked over and saw Enkidu standing there. Their eyes locked for a moment, and Gilgamesh had a curious look on his face. Enkidu stood and looked at the man he was supposed to defeat without blinking an eye. He didn't see evil in his eyes, and Enkidu began to wonder if it was all a mistake.

After a moment that seemed like a lifetime to Shamhat, Gilgamesh turned away from Enkidu and jumped off his horse. He approached Nergal and Ishara, who were both shaking in fear. Ishara didn't want to be with Gilgamesh. He wasn't Nergal, the man she married, and she didn't love him; more than this, she had heard the stories of how he treated his women. The legends of his physical abuse and strange sexual tendencies were well known, even among the townspeople. Enkidu turned to the old man beside him.

"What is he doing?" he asked the old man. The old man looked at Enkidu rather amusedly. How was it that anyone didn't know what was about to happen after so many years, the man thought? The old man snickered and answered Enkidu.

"He is going to take the bride for the night," he told him. Enkidu's face changed completely. He couldn't believe what he was hearing.

"What do you mean old man?" Enkidu asked.

"Are you thick in your skull or something?" the old man responded. "It is the law that the King will have the bride before her husband does. He does it with every new bride. It's the law."

"How can such a law exist?!" Enkidu huffed. He was becoming more agitated by the moment.

"I suppose it's rather convenient that Gilgamesh himself makes the laws," the old man chuckled. He elbowed Enkidu in the ribs as he said, "I guess if I made the laws, I would sleep with every beautiful woman too!"

"It is not right!" Enkidu sternly said to the old man.

"Well, tell it to the King," said the old man jokingly, as he smirked and pointed his finger toward Gilgamesh.

Enkidu looked over at Gilgamesh. His rage was beginning to build. He wasn't sure why he was so angry. It's true that it was not right what The King was doing, but he felt a blinding and uncontrollable rage beginning to form in his head. His hands balled up into fists and he began to shudder and shake with his anger. Suddenly, in that moment, he forgot what he thought just a moment ago; Gilgamesh *was* truly evil, and he needed to stop him from committing this unjust act on this innocent bride!

Gilgamesh grabbed Ishara by the arm and began to drag her toward his horse. She tried to struggle to get free, but Gilgamesh was far too strong. Nergal couldn't take it anymore, and he approached Gilgamesh, shouting for him to let her go. The crowd murmured in surprise. Gilgamesh threw Ishara to the ground and drew his sword. He put it to Nergal's throat. Nergal was deathly scared, and closed his eyes in fear. His breaths were short, his heart raced, and sweat was pouring from his brow.

"You dare to tell me what to do?" Gilgamesh asked calmly, twisting the sword. It began to cut into Nergal's throat, and blood was visibly running down Gilgamesh's sword tip.

"Please my King," Nergal answered meekly, still shaking with his fear and with tears running down his cheeks. "Please spare her."

Gilgamesh smirked maniacally, and then lowered his sword. Nergal thought it was all over for a moment, before Gilgamesh took the handle of the sword and smashed it into Nergal's face. He dropped to the ground in an instant. The entire side of his face was caved in, broken and shattered. There was blood spattered everywhere, even on the people who were standing several feet away. Ishara ran over to Nergal's side and wept. Enkidu's eyes grew wide as he watched Gilgamesh put his sword back in its scabbard, then grab Ishara again and drag her to his horse. He couldn't take anymore.

The King didn't even see it coming. With a lion's quickness, Enkidu leapt forward and smashed Gilgamesh in the head with his fist. He fell to the ground in astonishment. Ishara fell to the ground beside him. She quickly got up and ran back over to Nergal to see if he was all right. The people standing around the scene couldn't believe their eyes, and they let out an audible gasp. There had been no man in all of Sumeria who had ever even pushed Gilgamesh aside, let alone knocked him to the ground! Gilgamesh grabbed his chin in pain. He couldn't believe it either!

"I cannot allow you to perform this injustice to the people of Uruk any longer," Enkidu calmly told the King, standing over him. Gilgamesh stood to his feet and stared in wonder at this man. He was surprised because he didn't have to look down at this man, which was a first. Instead, he stood eye to eye with him. How could any man knock him to the ground, Gilgamesh wondered? The two stood, with their eyes locked, staring each other down. There was a hush over the crowd of people. Shamhat smiled and stepped out to the front of the herd, no longer hiding herself. Aruru, also, came out from where she had been concealing herself, and watched the show with a grin.

"Who are you?" Gilgamesh asked the strange man.

"I am Enkidu, of the forest," he answered slowly and deliberately. Gilgamesh already knew in his heart who he was though. His mother had warned him, and now the reality of her vision was standing right in front of him. There before him was a challenger of enormous strength to have knocked him down. For the first time in his life, Gilgamesh was unsure of what to do next.

"Why have you knocked me down Enkidu of the forest? Don't you know who I am?" Gilgamesh queried.

"I know exactly who you are King Gilgamesh," Enkidu answered. "And I have come from the Gods to stop your tyranny on the people of Uruk!"

"Tyranny? I see no tyranny here!" Gilgamesh mockingly said, looking about at his subjects. Each of them put their heads down as his eyes passed over them. "Why don't you go back to the forest and play with the animals good sir?"

"I'm not leaving until you renounce your throne, so your people can be free," Enkidu told him. Gilgamesh laughed in disbelief at what he was hearing. Enkidu stood his ground.

"But they are free," he said to Enkidu, with disdain in his voice. "They are free to do whatever they like…..so long as I allow it, of course." Gilgamesh chortled with a grin. "But you see, that is the nature of being a King. I don't expect some dirty scavenger like yourself to understand that."

"Then I will have to convince you with something other than words," Enkidu informed him. He took a step backward and bowed to Gilgamesh. Shullat and Gilgamesh's guards drew their swords.

"Put them back," Gilgamesh ordered his men. Shullat stared at Gilgamesh in disappointment, but finally put his sword back in its sheath. The other guards followed suit. "This fight is for me and me alone Shullat. Do not get involved!" Then Gilgamesh turned his attention back toward Enkidu.

"I am a God!" he proclaimed in a loud booming voice to Enkidu. "You are nothing but a filthy animal! And I will take care of you as I do all other animals I hunt and kill!"

Enkidu smiled, then stood up from his bowing position and waited. Gilgamesh drew his sword and pointed it at Enkidu. With a lunge, Gilgamesh ran forward at Enkidu, but hit nothing but air. He slashed and slashed at Enkidu, but he easily dodged each move with the quickness of a cat. Gilgamesh made one last lunge at him, but Enkidu jumped straight up into the air. Gilgamesh looked up and saw Enkidu sailing over him, then turned to see him land on the other side about 20 feet away. Enkidu smiled at Gilgamesh, who was standing with his mouth agape.

Before he could think about anything, Enkidu raced over to Gilgamesh like a gazelle, and picked him up.

Gilgamesh flailed his arms and legs, but Enkidu held on and threw him into the wall of the temple, about 100 feet away. The King impacted so hard that some of the Limestone wall cracked and pieces crumbled to the ground. Gilgamesh grabbed his back in pain, and stared over at his opponent, who was calmly standing and looking at him, waiting for his next move.

The King shouted in anger, and stepped forward to meet Enkidu again. Enkidu stood his ground once more. Gilgamesh moved forward slowly, until they were an arms' length away from each other. Enkidu still stood with a fixed gaze into Gilgamesh's eyes. Gilgamesh threw a punch, but Enkidu dodged it with lightning fast quickness. He threw another, but missed again. Then he tried to grab Enkidu and throw his arms around him, but Enkidu jumped into the air, bellowing a powerful roar, like that of a lion. Gilgamesh stared up at him sailing over him again. It seemed he was floating in the sky. He must have jumped 30 feet into the air and over Gilgamesh. The crowd of people gasped at the spectacle. He landed several feet away, then turned and smiled at the King again. Gilgamesh was still a bit stunned at what this man could do. Enkidu took the opportunity, and leapt into the air with his feet first. He smashed into Gilgamesh's chest and sent him flying backward into a nearby tree. The tree broke in the middle and the top half bent over at a 45 degree angle. Gilgamesh again grabbed his back and head in pain. Even though the pain was great, Gilgamesh was becoming agitated and more and more angry by the moment. He approached Enkidu again, who was again, calmly waiting for him.

"You must be from the Gods, I must admit that," Gilgamesh told his opponent, still rubbing the back of his head in pain. "And I knew you were coming for me, Enkidu of the forest. But there is one thing you should know."

"And what is that?" inquired Enkidu.

"You may match my strength and power, but there is one thing you *don't* have."

"And what is that?" he repeated.

Gilgamesh threw a kick at Enkidu, who leapt into the air to avoid it. At the same moment, Gilgamesh jumped up straight into the air as well and intercepted him, knocking Enkidu to the ground. He landed with a thud.

"You don't have my intellect, animal," Gilgamesh told him triumphantly. Enkidu was now the one wincing in pain this time. Gilgamesh walked over to him and picked him up over his head. "It's what separates man from beast," he told him emphatically. He threw Enkidu into the same tree that Gilgamesh himself had hit before. This time the tree broke completely in half. Enkidu fell on his back to the ground and didn't move.

"No!" Shamhat cried out. Gilgamesh turned his head to see Shamhat standing there. She looked up at him and began to slowly back away. He hadn't noticed her before this moment.

"Shamhat?" asked Gilgamesh, surprised to see her face. Shamhat stopped in her tracks. "Where have you been?"

"I.....I......" she stammered, while slowly backing away again from the King.

"Why are you backing away from me?" Gilgamesh asked her, holding out his arms to her. Shamhat didn't answer. She was shaking with fear. Looking over in the direction of Enkidu, she could see he was still motionless. Then Gilgamesh looked over at Enkidu, then back at Shamhat. A look of clarity came over his face. He finally understood why she was acting the way she was. Gilgamesh's arms dropped to his sides. His eyes narrowed and he glared at Shamhat. Her heart felt as though it would jump out of her chest. She looked over to try to find Aruru. She had disappeared into the crowd again.

"Is this animal with you?!" he asked Shamhat sternly, yet amusedly. She didn't answer. Gilgamesh slowly approached Shamhat. She covered her head with her arms and crouched on the ground, waiting to be pummeled. Suddenly Gilgamesh could hear the crowd gasping again. He looked back to see Enkidu holding the entire top half of the broken tree in his arms. The King's jaw dropped and eyes widened in surprise. Enkidu swung and hit Gilgamesh plainly in the chest with the tree. It flung him back several hundred feet onto the ground. Gilgamesh coughed and gasped for breath as he tried to get up again. He tasted something in his mouth. It was strange. The King put two fingers on his tongue and then removed them. He could see blood! He had never bled before! Gilgamesh spit out the taste from his mouth, and out came more of the red mocking color. Enkidu would pay for that, he told himself!

His body was sore, and in more pain than he had ever felt in his life, but he steadied himself upright. He picked up a large rock in each hand, and then approached Enkidu again. Enkidu threw down the tree and waited for him to come. The crowd was thoroughly enjoying the battle. They had never seen anything like it. "Ooohs" and "Ahhhs" filled the air whenever the two men attacked. Shamhat's demeanor had suddenly changed when Enkidu struck Gilgamesh with the tree, and she was now standing up again and cheering her champion on.

Gilgamesh came closer to Enkidu, still grasping the boulders in each hand. When Gilgamesh was a few feet away, he flung one of the rocks at Enkidu with all his might. Enkidu leapt into the air to avoid it, and landed on top of the temple roof. The boulder landed against the wall of the temple and smashed into pieces. Gilgamesh threw the other rock at Enkidu up on the roof, but he jumped down just as quickly to avoid it. Then Gilgamesh revealed another small rock he had been concealing in his belt around his waist. With inhuman precision, he hurled it at Enkidu as he landed on the ground. It found its mark, and Enkidu fell to the ground, wounded by the projectile. The left side of his head was cut and bleeding badly. Gilgamesh let out a grunt and grasped his own side, for he was still in a lot of pain himself, but he proceeded to walk over to where Enkidu was. From a distance, Enkidu appeared to be unconscious, and was not moving. Shamhat put her hands over her mouth, and tears streamed out of her eyes and down her cheeks. Gilgamesh stared at her as he passed by where she was standing and then continued over to where Enkidu lay.

Just as he came close to him, he bent over to examine whether Enkidu was alive or dead. With the speed of a leopard, Enkidu grasped Gilgamesh's neck with his legs and squeezed like a python. Gilgamesh tried to separate Enkidu's legs from around his neck, but he could not pry apart the powerful tree trunk like limbs. He gasped for breath as Enkidu continued to squeeze the life out of the King. Gilgamesh picked up Enkidu's body in his arms and slowly walked over to the wall of the temple behind them. Enkidu's legs were still wrapped around his neck, and his body was sticking out parallel to the ground and perpendicular from Gilgamesh's body.

Gilgamesh pivoted his body and then swung Enkidu's torso into the wall of the temple. Enkidu cried out in pain, but held onto his grip. Gilgamesh was running short of breath, but he swung Enkidu into the wall again, desperately trying to free himself. Enkidu's arm and side began to bleed as the wall cut into his flesh. Still, he did not let go of his hold. He was determined to choke Gilgamesh into submission, or even death if need be! Gilgamesh flailed his arms around, and then fell to the ground on his side. Enkidu held on for dear life. He could feel Gilgamesh growing weaker as he struggled for breath. It seemed that The King was fading, and Shamhat cheered for her champion to finish him. Aruru whistled and giggled as she could see the end of Gilgamesh's reign in her mind. The crowd had been very much divided during the fight. Most of them secretly cheered for Enkidu, but a few of them were truly concerned for Gilgamesh; including Shullat.

Shullat had stood by and watched the amazing fight long enough on The King's orders, but now he felt he needed to do something. He grabbed his sword and approached Enkidu and Gilgamesh, still both tangled on the ground. When he was right above Enkidu, he dangled his sword above his head, and grasped it with both hands firmly. Just before he was about to thrust it down, and plunge it into Enkidu's torso, Enkidu let go of his grasp on Gilgamesh. He flung Shullat back with a quick kick in the chest. Shullat dropped his sword and fell to the ground with a thud. He was completely knocked out.

Enkidu leapt to his feet, but Gilgamesh, freed from his grip, was waiting. He punched Enkidu in the chest and flung him back several feet into the wall of the temple. Enkidu staggered forward, covered in blood. He tried to leap into the air, but Gilgamesh anticipated his move and caught his legs as he went up. Enkidu smashed down to the ground and Gilgamesh picked him up and flung him against a nearby rock. You could hear the bones of Enkidu's ribs crack as he hit the rock on his right side. He collapsed to the ground and did not move.

Gilgamesh sighed in relief, then grabbed his own sides and bent over in pain. As the adrenaline of battle began to wear off, he began to feel his own wounds more and more. Gilgamesh sat down on the ground in front of the temple's entrance and gasped for air. His neck still bore red marks from where he was being strangled to near death by Enkidu, and he spit out some more blood from his mouth. He was breathing deeply in exhaustion. Gilgamesh looked back up and saw that Enkidu had still not yet moved. He hoped it would last this time.

The King turned his head gingerly and looked around into the crowd. They were all staring in awe at what they had witnessed. Many of them turned their eyes away from The King, knowing they had cheered for his defeat. But it was only one person in particular that he was looking for; Shamhat. She had disappeared again, like a morning mist being chased away by the sun. Aruru too had fled when Enkidu had hit the rock and been knocked out.

Gilgamesh had never been in such pain in his entire life. Not one man in all Sumeria, Assyria, or Egypt could ever do what this man had done to him. This man was surely the man his mother warned him about; a man from the Gods. Shullat was still lying on his back on the ground. Gilgamesh looked at him for a moment. If it had not been for his distraction, he very well could have lost to Enkidu; and he knew it! All of the anger he had felt toward Enkidu in the beginning was fading as he sat on the ground in agony. For the first time in his life he truly felt the sting of battle; what other mere mortal men must have felt when they fought and were injured, or even killed. He could have been killed this day, and the thought had never before even occurred to him. Today it was real for the first time. His mortality was real for the first time.     Gilgamesh limped over to Enkidu who was barely beginning to stir. Gilgamesh felt remorse that he had to inflict such pain on such a worthy adversary. It was the first time he ever had felt remorse. For that matter, it was the first time he was concerned for the life of any person he had fought. The King truly hoped that Enkidu would not die. As he stood over him and watched him struggle to regain consciousness, he had the strangest feeling about him. Though he had never met him before this day, it was as if he had always known this man. He seemed almost familiar. It seemed like there was an intrinsic connection between the two of them. Gilgamesh couldn't explain the feeling, but it was very real; as if it had been put in his heart by the Gods themselves.

Enkidu opened his eyes and saw Gilgamesh standing over him. He was still a bit groggy and in terrible pain. It felt as though an entire mountain had crashed down onto his body. Trying to move, Enkidu grimaced and fell back. He tried to make it up to a sitting position, but his badly bruised body fell back to the ground each time he tried. Enkidu stared up hazily at Gilgamesh. The King stared back for a moment, and then extended his hand out to him. There was a silence; it seemed like forever. The people gathered around all waited anxiously to see if Enkidu would accept the King's hand. Finally, after what seemed like an eternity, Enkidu slowly extended his own hand, and Gilgamesh grabbed his arm, pulling him up to a standing position. Enkidu was still a bit shaky, and struggled to stand. Gilgamesh steadied him by putting Enkidu's arm around his shoulder. Gilgamesh grimaced, himself still sore and bleeding from the battle.

"I admit defeat to you Gilgamesh," Enkidu whispered to him meekly. Gilgamesh looked at Enkidu a moment, and then broke out in laughter. When he did, he grabbed his side with his free arm and spit up a wad of blood. Enkidu couldn't help but start to laugh himself at the spectacle, but his laughter also caused him intense pain. The two of them fell down to the ground and sat, interspersing laughter with shrieks of pain and agony. Neither of them was sure why they were laughing at such a moment, but it seemed appropriate somehow. It was truly a sight to behold. The townspeople of Uruk weren't sure what to make of it all. They were all scratching their heads and murmuring to each other.

"I'm not sure why I am laughing," Gilgamesh said, snickering. Enkidu shrugged his shoulders and continued to cackle.

"Me neither," Enkidu finally answered in between laughs.

"By the way, I'm Gilgamesh, King of Sumeria," he told Enkidu, then chortled some more.

"Nice to meet you Gilgamesh," he told him. "I am Enkidu, of the forest."

Enkidu smiled. Gilgamesh also smiled, and the two continued to revel in the sudden comradery they felt toward each other. Then Gilgamesh and Enkidu stopped laughing and got serious for a moment.

"Anyway, I was sent here by the Gods," Enkidu said. "At least, I think I was."

"I know," Gilgamesh replied. Enkidu looked surprised. "I have been waiting for you a long time."

"Waiting for me? How did you know that I was coming?" Enkidu asked.

"My mother," he told him. "She is the Goddess Nininsina, The Goddess of Fertility. Because of her blessings, the land here in Sumeria is always fertile."

"Then you *are* a God?" Enkidu curiously asked.

"Half, actually," replied Gilgamesh.

"No wonder you are so powerful," Enkidu said, now pondering the wisdom of trying to fight a God.

"Were you with Shamhat?" Gilgamesh inquired. Enkidu looked up at him in surprise. "Because I saw her standing in the crowd and cheering you on."

"Yes, I guess I am; or was. I'm not quite sure now. I notice she is gone." Enkidu began to look about in the crowd, but like Gilgamesh, found no trace of her.

"Yes, she is," said Gilgamesh, rubbing his chin. "Typical of Shamhat. She uses a person only to try to get what she wants. When she saw you had lost, she fled. Any noble woman would have stood by you and accepted your defeat as her own, but not Shamhat! I would expect no less from her."

"I should have known as well," Enkidu said, shaking his head. "She told me that it was my destiny to come here and face you Gilgamesh. She said she had a vision from the Gods. I should have known better than to trust her."

"That part is probably true," Gilgamesh told Enkidu. "She often did have visions that proved to later be true. She always claimed they came from the Goddess Ishtar, a little obsession of hers; well, besides trying to seduce me into taking her for my Queen! Anyway, she was correct that you were to come here to meet me. My mother saw the same vision, and she is *never* wrong."

"Why? Why is *this* my destiny?" Enkidu asked rhetorically. "I was quite happy in the forest with the animals!" He put his hands up to his forehead and wept. "The human world is still strange to me, even after these months of living in it. I feel lost."

Gilgamesh watched as tears began to form in his eyes, and something in him was moved by the honest expression of emotion that Enkidu had. There was no pretense to this man; he said and expressed whatever he felt. There were times in Gilgamesh's life, like the death of his mother, that he wished to weep as well, but he could not. It wasn't the sort of thing a King should do; or a God for that matter! He felt true pity for Enkidu in his heart. It was another first.

"I'm sorry Enkidu," Gilgamesh said, looking up into the sky. The sun was beginning to set, and the sky was turning that reddish color that he loved so much. "It is my fault that you are here; that you were ripped from your home and put through this trial."

"What do you mean?" asked Enkidu, a bit confused at this revelation. Gilgamesh was silent for a moment. He put his head down and sighed in resignation.

"I *have* been less that noble in my Kingdom," he admitted for the first time. It was not only an admission to Enkidu, but to himself as well. "I have ruled my subjects with injustice and fear. I have tortured innocent men for pleasure and killed women and children without remorse. Everything my mother taught me in my youth about being noble like my Father, I have done the opposite in my arrogance and conceit."

"That still doesn't explain why it is your fault I am here," Enkidu informed him. Gilgamesh nodded his head and continued.

"It is because of this behavior, for so many years, that the people of Uruk cried out to Anu. He sent you here to me." Gilgamesh explained.

"Why?"

"I thought I knew. I honestly thought that you would be the one to defeat me in battle. It was the greatest fear in my heart that I would lose everything and be killed by the man sent from the Gods to challenge me! But, now.....I don't know. I have been victorious, and yet......"

"Yet what?" asked Enkidu, putting his hand on Gilgamesh's shoulder.

"I think I finally realize that you were never meant to kill me or defeat me in battle. If it were the will of the Gods, then I wouldn't be alive now." Gilgamesh turned and looked at Enkidu. "Maybe the reason you are here was to teach me something. Something I needed to learn."

"What's that?" Enkidu asked. Gilgamesh turned and looked into the sunset.

"Humility," Gilgamesh said, letting out a sigh. "For the first time in my life I am honestly looking at all the bad things I have done; and I feel ashamed! I don't know, but it seems that you are, I don't know, maybe my opposite or something. You are a pure being of right and good, and you, somehow, complete something that is missing in me. Does that make sense?"

"Yes. In fact it does," Enkidu said, grinning and nodding his head. He looked up into the sky. "The reddish color is peaceful, don't you think Gilgamesh?"

"Yes. I've always thought so," he answered.

The two men sat and watched the sun set over Sumeria. The townspeople dispersed and settled back into their homes, still murmuring under their breaths about what had happened. It was uncertain what the outcome of this battle was to them, but they had come to learn that anything was possible under this King. Enkidu and Gilgamesh both felt the first peace they had since their destinies had put them on a collision course. One had been victorious. One had suffered defeat; but in the end, they had both found something in each other that they had lacked. And maybe now, together, they would find a better future for Uruk.

# Tablet three

*"The fox could not build his own house, and so he came to the house of his friend as a conqueror............"*

Siduri couldn't believe what she had done. It was a hasty decision, but one that she felt she had to make under the circumstances. The only one who knew was Delondra. She wasn't quite sure she could trust her, but Delondra had caught her in the act, and decided, albeit begrudgingly, to help her. Siduri could trust no one now. All the other servants hated her, her father disowned her in his heart, and Gilgamesh.......well, after what happened, she just couldn't be with him anymore. It was too dangerous. However, it was equally dangerous to do what she had just done. Where would she go now? How would she live?

After the horrible events of the past evening had become clear in her mind again, Siduri had decided there was no other choice than to flee. She couldn't risk the life of her child at the hands of Gilgamesh. He didn't even know that she was pregnant with his child, but yet he had struck her with such force as to knock her out and nearly kill her; and all this over a simple flirting with Shullat! She hadn't meant anything by it, but Gilgamesh had taken it all wrong. What would he do when he found out that she was carrying an heir? Her father was probably right that he would kill her and her baby!

While Gilgamesh and all of the other servants had left to attend the wedding ceremony of Nergal and Ishara, she had silently left her chambers. There were few guards left in the Palace as many of them were with Gilgamesh to assure his security, though this was probably not necessary anyway. Siduri took the opportunity nonetheless, and snuck down the steps to the main chamber of the Palace. All of the servants' quarters were located on the second floor, except for Gilgamesh's chamber. It was the only room on the third floor, and it was lavishly huge. His bedroom was half the size of the entire second floor, which housed more than 20 servant quarters. To walk across Gilgamesh's bedroom actually took some time, especially for someone as small as Siduri.

Delondra had caught her sneaking down and preparing to leave the Palace. At first, she had tried to stop her, but when Siduri revealed why she had found her that night in such a horrid condition, Delondra had agreed to hide Siduri; especially for the safety of her innocent child. In any case, Siduri was hardly in the condition to have fled anywhere to safety. She could still barely walk and had awful headaches. Delondra took her to her cousin's home, just at the edge of the city of Kish, to the north of Uruk. No one was allowed to leave the palace without Gilgamesh's permission. It would be considered a crime for Siduri to go as she did, and despite his affection for her, she could be executed if she were caught.

Her cousin was apprehensive about taking her in. If it became known that she was keeping Siduri there, surely Gilgamesh would burn her home to the ground and throw her in prison! It was bad enough that her husband had already been killed during Gilgamesh's invasion of Uruk. Her husband had been a soldier for Dumuzi, and had been shown no mercy when captured by some of Gilgamesh's troops. It was due to this fact that Delondra's cousin ultimately said yes to Siduri though. She also had a grudge to bear against the King.

Irkalla was the name of Delondra's cousin, though they looked as though they could be sisters to Siduri. Both of them were tall and very skinny, and had the same shape of face. However, Irkalla was a bit less odd than Delondra. While Delondra spoke in a wispy, odd voice, and was obsessed with charms, visions, and spiritual things, Irkalla was very down-to-earth and grounded in reality.

It's not to say that maybe there wasn't something to Delondra's ranting though. After all, she did know that she was pregnant when no one else did. But Irkalla was much more practical. When Delondra turned 18, which would be in about a month or so, she would be released from the harem, and she had already planned to come and stay with Irkalla. Delondra's parents didn't want her back, so Irkalla had offered to take her in.

Siduri found that she got along well with Irkalla, but she was also very nervous about Gilgamesh finding her. As soon as she had come to stay with Irkalla, the news had already spread about the city of the epic battle between Gilgamesh and this stranger from the forest. Siduri was shocked to learn about it, but not surprised. She had been one of the few people who knew about the visions his mother had seen, and it made perfect sense that it had come to pass. It just seemed a bit ironic that it happened at this particular time for Siduri. But in any case, it was probably a good thing. Perhaps Gilgamesh would be preoccupied enough to not search for her any time soon.

A month passed by and Siduri began to show her pregnancy. She was unable to hide it anymore, but with the fear in her mind of Gilgamesh finding her fading each day, she stayed in Kish. She had no problem now embracing her condition. Siduri was hoping for a son. Not simply because boys were more highly valued than girls in Sumerian society, but because he would be heir to Gilgamesh's throne someday. What a shock it would be to the King when his son came calling one day to take the throne from him. It would be the perfect irony; and justice for that matter!

Delondra, after returning to the Palace the month before, had finally been released of her obligations as a concubine. While she was in the palace for the last month, however, she had learned that Gilgamesh was forming a search party to look for Siduri. He was assigning some of his finest soldiers to the task. Delondra decided she must warn Siduri as soon as she returned to Irkalla's. He was determined to find her and get her back. The truth was that he had been happier with her than Shamhat, or any other woman before. It had been a horrible lack in judgment to hit her that night, but he had been enraged when he saw her flirting with Shullat. He couldn't fault Shullat for it; he was a man after all. Any man could hardly resist a beautiful woman's sexual advances. It was in their nature, he concluded. But a woman should be able to control herself, and he was still disappointed in her, though this hardly dissuaded him from wanting her back.

Irkalla was talented at sewing garments, and she was able to weave together clothes for the baby to be. They weren't the lavish materials that Siduri had experienced in the Palace, but because of Irkalla's fine craftsmanship, it was hardly noticeable. After returning to the house to stay, Delondra had repeatedly come to Siduri's room in the middle of the night to convey the many weird visions she was having about the baby. Siduri decided that it was best to humor Delondra and just agree to whatever she was saying. She wasn't quite sure if anything Delondra had seen would come true, but Siduri found that if she didn't simply nod her head and say "oh really", and "that's interesting" a lot, Delondra would never leave her room and let her sleep in peace.

All of the "visions" that Delondra had seen thus far, though, had been positive. She would have a boy, and he would grow quite tall and powerful, like his father. One day he *would* rule Uruk in Gilgamesh's place and Siduri would return to Uruk when this happened, and reclaim her life of privilege that she felt she deserved for carrying the Son of a God. Siduri desperately wanted to believe that Delondra could truly foresee the future, and that it would happen just as she had predicted, but given the circumstance, she decided it was highly doubtful. She couldn't continue to hide from Gilgamesh forever. One day he would probably find her, whether he searched for her himself, or someone in the town that was still loyal to the King, turned her in. It was a distinct advantage that most of the people of Kish despised Gilgamesh, for Kish had once been the power center of Sumeria.

It was Gilgamesh who had decided to make Uruk his new home, and it was shortly after, that Gilgamesh had seized control. Many of the people still remembered the prosperity that Kish enjoyed when it was the seat of power in the region, and many were still bitter that it had moved to Uruk. What's more, many of them still loved Dumuzi and hated Gilgamesh for overthrowing him. Still, it remained a possible threat that someone in town could turn her in, so she tried to stay indoors as much as possible.

One morning, Irkalla was preparing a meal for them all, when Delondra burst into the home. It appeared that she had been running, or something. She was out of breath and had a very worried look on her face.

"What is the matter?" Irkalla asked Delondra. Delondra slammed shut the front door of the dwelling. She continued to stand in front of the door and didn't answer Irkalla's question. Irkalla stopped preparing the food, and came over to where Delondra was standing. Siduri also got up from where she had been sitting and went over to see if Delondra was all right.

"Tell us what is wrong Delondra?" Siduri said to her again. Delondra did not move. She hung her head down and breathed in deeply. Irkalla came over and put her hand on Delondra's shoulder. Siduri came to the other side and put her hand on the other shoulder.

"Come on, let's sit down, all of us," Irkalla said, and then proceeded to pry Delondra's hand from the door. Siduri followed suit, and the two of them walked Delondra away from the door. The three women sat down on the floor cross-legged.

"Now tell us what this is all about," Siduri said to Delondra. She didn't move or speak. Delondra looked pale, as though she had seen a spirit or something. Irkalla got up and went to the other room to fetch Delondra some water. Siduri continued her attempt to reach her. "Please, Delondra. You must tell us what is wrong so we can help you."

"You can't help," Delondra said softly. She began to shake and tremble. Irkalla returned with the water, but Delondra was too unstable to drink any. The cup fell to the floor as Irkalla tried to give some to her. Delondra began to shake more and more. Siduri took her hand and tried to calm her, but the shaking was becoming out of control. Delondra's eyes rolled back as she fell to the floor and began to twitch. Irkalla and Siduri both looked at each other in panic. Neither knew what was going on. Delondra was saying something under her breath. Neither Irkalla nor Siduri could make out what she was saying, but It sounded like another language altogether. It seemed as if she had been possessed by a demon or something. A strange green substance began to come out of Delondra's mouth as she continued to shudder on the floor. Suddenly, Delondra let out a scream, like a scream of pain and agony. Then, just as suddenly as it had started, it stopped. Delondra's body lay lifeless on the floor of Irkalla's home, motionless. Siduri and Irkalla gathered enough courage to approach her seemingly lifeless body.

"Delondra?" asked Irkalla, almost in a whisper. Siduri too tried to rouse her by calling her name, but Delondra continued to lay there, unresponsive.

"What do we do now?" Siduri asked, frightened by what had just happened.

"I don't know," Irkalla responded, equally shaken. She had been just as freaked out by the display. As the two women looked at each other in disbelief and confusion, Delondra suddenly sat up and looked around the room. Stunned, Siduri and Irkalla stared at Delondra, who was acting as though nothing had happened.

"Delondra!" Irkalla exclaimed. She looked at Irkalla and wondered why she was acting so funny.

"How do you feel?" asked Siduri to Delondra. She shrugged her shoulders and answered, "Fine."

"You scared us half to death!" Irkalla said. Delondra looked confusedly at Irkalla, and then looked around the room again. "I am thirsty," she said. Irkalla looked at her for a second, and then got up again to fetch another cup of water. Delondra was sweating from her ordeal, so Siduri grabbed a piece of cloth and began to wipe the sweat from Delondra's brow. Delondra looked at her and cocked her head to one side.

"What are you doing?" she asked in a befuddled tone. Siduri didn't look up, she continued to dab her forehead with the cloth. Irkalla came back with the water, and Delondra took a sip.

"Do you remember what just happened?" Irkalla asked Delondra. She cocked her head to the other side this time looked at her cousin.

"What are you talking about?" she said to Irkalla. Siduri finished wiping up the mess on the floor, and then got up to throw the cloth away.

"You were writhing on the floor like a snake just a second ago!" Irkalla exclaimed. "Don't you remember?"

"No. I just remember that I was outside picking some flowers from your garden. Then I was here, sitting on the floor"

"You mean, you don't remember anything?" Siduri asked her.

"No. Now tell me what is going on," Delondra said to her with a firm voice.

"You came in the door in a panic!" Irkalla told her. Delondra listened with a confused look on her face. "You didn't want to move from the door. Then we sat you down, and I went to get you water."

"And then you started to shake uncontrollably," Siduri added. Delondra continued to look at the two in disbelief. How could all this have happened without her knowledge? It seemed ridiculous. On the other hand, she didn't know how she wound up on the floor of the house when she had just been standing in the garden outside. It was all very confusing.

"What were you doing in the garden anyway?" Irkalla asked Delondra.

"Is that all you're worried about right now?!" Siduri asked in a scolding tone to Irkalla.

"Well….," was all she responded, shrugging her shoulders. Delondra often went out and picked some of the flowers in Irkalla's garden because they were pretty. It drove Irkalla insane because she was very particular about how her garden looked. When Delondra picked some of the flowers, it didn't balance out anymore, and there were visible holes in the line of beautiful flowers that Irkalla had planted. "I think there are bigger issues here," Siduri said to Irkalla.

"I know," Irkalla said. "It's just that my garden…"

"Would someone like to tell me what's going on?" Delondra said, breaking into the two women's kibitzing.

"Sorry," Irkalla and Siduri told her in unison.

"Well, I don't remember a thing after the garden," Delondra told them.

"You were mumbling something," Siduri told her. Delondra cocked her head to the side again. It was something she seemed to always do when she was confused. "It was strange; like, another language of some kind."

"Really?" Delondra asked.

"Yeah," added Irkalla. "It almost sounded like Egyptian or something. I don't know, but it wasn't Sumerian!"

"That's strange," Delondra said in her wispy voice. Siduri and Irkalla looked at each other in wonder. It didn't seem that she was upset about it at all. She had just experienced something out of this world, and she acted as though it happened every day!

"Why don't you go and rest a bit," Irkalla told Delondra. She nodded her head, then got up and went to the other room to sleep. Irkalla got up and pulled back the thick blanket sheet that separated the doorway to the two rooms so she could speak to Siduri without Delondra hearing her.

"What in the name of Anu was all that about?" Siduri whispered to Irkalla. Irkalla shrugged her shoulders and sat down next to Siduri.

"Who knows? But after all these years, I have come to expect strange things from that girl. Even when she was a child, she talked about "visions" and "spirits". It drove her mother absolutely batty." Siduri looked over at the blanket to make sure that Delondra wasn't listening. Irkalla tapped Siduri's hand, and then continued. "You know, her parents even brought in an Ashipu to look at her once, because they believed she was possessed by demons!"

"I know. Delondra said something about it when she first took care of me."

"They also brought in the local Asu to look at her, but neither could do anything for her. After some time, her parents gave up trying," Irkalla said. "That's when Gilgamesh took her for the harem." Irkalla leaned over to Siduri and whispered in her ear, "Her parents were actually *relieved* when Gilgamesh took her!"

"So, do you really believe in all that stuff?" Siduri asked. Irkalla raised her eyebrow and shrugged her shoulders.

"Who knows? Maybe she really can see the future. Maybe we're all crazy and she is the sane one."

"Think so?" Siduri said. Irkalla looked at Siduri with serious eyes, and then burst out laughing.

"No way!" she said, giggling. Siduri giggled a bit herself, and then got serious again.

"But what about what we just saw?" she asked Irkalla. "What was that then?"

"Who knows? Maybe it's something to do with her health or something. You saw the way she was shaking on the floor; something just isn't right. She must be sick or something."

"Maybe you're right," said Siduri. Irkalla got up and went to check on Delondra. She pulled back the sheet, and peered in. Delondra was lying down with her eyes closed. Irkalla went back and put her hands up to her lips. Siduri got the message, and the two headed outside to see what damage Delondra had done to the garden this time.

As the two women left, Delondra sat up and sighed. She stared out of the window outside and thought about what had just happened. This sort of thing always used to happen when she lived with her parents, but it had stopped for a long time. They had come to get used to it by the time she was a teenager, but Irkalla and Siduri were clearly a little freaked out by it all. Why was it she had to be cursed with these gifts, she wondered? Sometimes she felt special because she could see things and was open to the spirits, but most of the time it was a burden.

People often acted strangely around her, as if they didn't even want to be in the same room. It had happened many times in the harem that she had woken up and had other concubines tell her that she had been sleepwalking, or mumbling in her sleep. She often had told the other women of her visions, but all of them blew her off as a bit of a mental case. Most people thought she was just plain strange, and avoided her completely. Gilgamesh chose her only for her beauty, but she suspected that if he knew about her strange demeanor, he would have let her go a long time ago from the Harem. In fact, there had been a few times when she was with him that she had seen quick visions of things to come; the same ones his mother had seen, but she didn't tell him, for fear he would send her home. She didn't want to return home. There, her parents treated her like a freak; and she actually *enjoyed* being a concubine. At least there, someone desired to be in her company now and then!

Delondra got up and walked out into the other room. She could hear Siduri and Irkalla talking just outside the door about what to do with her. She wondered if she should tell them about what she had seen during her episode on the floor. She *had* been conscious while in that state, though it wasn't apparent to Siduri and Irkalla. She had played dumb to them about not knowing what happened. It wasn't the first time it had happened either. Her most vivid visions came during these episodes, and the one she had just seen was terrifying!

She stood for a moment and listened, then went back to her room to sleep. It probably wouldn't have done any good, she thought to herself. Who was going to listen to a freak anyway?

-------------------------------------------------------------

After a few months time, Gilgamesh had become bored; so had Enkidu for that matter. Enkidu longed to be back in the forest with the animals again. It was a simpler life, without the constant politics of the humans to deal with. Things in nature were just what they were. In the human world, there was much pretense and jockeying for position. People always weren't what they seemed, and often they lied and deceived to get what they wanted. Often people would be your friend to your face, but talk ill of you as soon as you turned your back. It was a depressing way of life, Enkidu had decided.

Nonetheless, he enjoyed his friendship with Gilgamesh very much, and had happily watched as Gilgamesh softened many of his ways with his people after their battle. Though he had lost the battle with Gilgamesh, he found he may have won the war. The new self-reflective King was a far cry from who he used to be, just as his mother had told him. He still maintained strict control, but he no longer tortured, for he felt it was too cruel; he no longer slept with the bride of any man he wished, but instead, kept his sexual encounters to members of his harem; even in the harem, he had allowed those women who wanted to leave, to leave. Some of them had, but some of them had stayed, feeling it was still a better life than they had come from. Many times Gilgamesh had offered to Enkidu one of his beautiful concubines, but Enkidu was still pining for Shamhat. He didn't know why. She had used him, in a way, to try to exact revenge on Gilgamesh in a self-serving manner. He did believe that she had been led to him by the Gods, but her motives weren't true to what the Gods wanted, but to her own selfish agenda. Despite all of this though, he still loved her and dreamed of her. Shamhat hadn't shown her face anywhere since the incident, despite Gilgamesh's and Enkidu's efforts to try to find her. It was as if she disappeared off the face of the world.

Despite the peace that the townspeople now enjoyed under the "new" reign of Gilgamesh, there were still troubles on the horizon. Pharaoh Khasekemwy of Egypt was a constant threat as he built up his own army to match the great army of Sumeria. Shullat had many spies that had told him of Khasekemwy's obsession with uniting the power of the Egyptian empire with that of the Sumerians, thus having all consuming power in the world. To date, the Egyptians had never been able to match the might of the Sumerians, though they came close under Dumuzi's reign. In fact, many of the Egyptian people believed that if Seth-Peribsen and Dumuzi had not struck a peace deal, the Egyptians could have taken over the Sumerian empire. Both of the rulers had opted for peace instead at the time. But now with the two very aggressive and ambitious rulers in Gilgamesh and Khasekemwy, who knew what would happen?

And then there were the Assyrians in the west. They had already mounted an offensive before Enkidu came to Uruk. Even though it was unsuccessful, the Assyrians *always* had an underground army of disenfranchised people who wanted to fight Gilgamesh. Even as Enkidu helped Gilgamesh find peace in his own heart, and peaceful times for his subjects, the Assyrians already had chosen a new leader for their rebellion; Sargon. Rumor had it that he had started a very ambitious and foolish campaign to enter the cedar forests of Lebanon.

At the border of Lebanon, in the far west, there were dense forests that separated the Lebanese from the rest of the world. These forests were even thicker and more dangerous than the forest north of the Zagros Mountains, that Enkidu had lived in. No man could tame the forest, except for the Lebanese, and even they could only enter a hundred yards or so into it, on the west side where they lived. But the cedar there was the finest wood in the entire world, and the Lebanese counted on it for trade. Without it, they would surely perish.

The forest also acted as protection for the Lebanese. There was only one route out of Lebanon without crossing the forest, and it was heavily guarded by their army. Being able to condense their army to protect only one road made it nearly impossible for any army to invade them, even vast ones like the Egyptians. However, anyone who could conquer the Lebanese and control the entire cedar forest would command riches and power in the world. Sargon was hoping that if he could take control of the forest, he could build an army with the forest riches that would overthrow Gilgamesh.

One day, Shullat ran into the Palace, and straight up to Gilgamesh's chamber. He could hear all the way from down the hallway that Gilgamesh was there with one of his concubines, and Shullat didn't want to disturb him. Coming back down the stairs to the second floor, he went down one of the elaborate hallways to Enkidu's room. Enkidu was there, standing and staring out of his window.

"I'm not disturbing you, am I Enkidu?" Shullat asked him, breaking Enkidu's thoughts. He looked over at Shullat and shook his head.

"No Shullat. Please come in and sit," Enkidu invited. Shullat sat down on a wooden chair by Enkidu's bed. Enkidu continued to stand. He could never quite get used to sitting much. It seemed awkward, even after all this time. When he lived in the forest, he almost never sat. He was always moving with the animals, finding water, hunting food, or protecting his territory; the only time he stopped was to sleep.

"I have just heard something from one of my Assyrian spies that troubles me," he said to Enkidu. Enkidu looked intrigued.

"Have you already told Gilgamesh?" Enkidu asked him. Shullat shook his head.

"He is.....busy, with one of his concubines." Enkidu nodded in understanding.

"Tell me what it is that is troubling you then?" Enkidu said.

"They tell me that Sargon is on his way to Lebanon right now as we speak," Shullat stated. Enkidu narrowed his eyes in confusion.

"Why would he do that?" asked Enkidu, pacing the floor. It was a habit he couldn't control. He always needed to be moving.

"Because he is trying to be the thousandth person who thought he could cut down the cedar forest and conquer the Lebanese!" Shullat jokingly told him.

"It is suicide!" exclaimed Enkidu. Shullat nodded. "Why is it you are so concerned then Shullat? Do you think that Sargon can actually accomplish this?" Shullat grabbed his stomach as he laughed out loud in response.

"Of course not!" he Chortled. "He could barely conquer an army of Sumerian children with the resources he has!"

"Then why are you telling me this?" Enkidu inquired, waiting for Shullat to stop laughing.

"Well, I was just thinking….." Shullat began.

"About what?"

"There are many rumors about the Cedar Forest. That it's much more dangerous to cross the forest than to fight the Lebanese," Shullat said.

"And of what consequence is this to us?" Enkidu queried.

"Well, I've always wondered if these rumors are really true," Shullat said to Enkidu. Enkidu looked puzzled. "You see, it is true that if anyone could control and cut down the Cedar forest, they would have, possibly, the greatest resource of trade and wealth in the world."

"And you think that *Gilgamesh* should be the one to cut it down?" Enkidu said, stopping his pacing for the moment.

"Well, yes, why not?" Shullat said, pausing as he rose up out of his chair and walked to the window. "But my concern is of this myth about the forest. It's not the Lebanese army that concerns me; it is the stories and legends."

"Stories and legends?" said Enkidu.

"Yes. In Sumerian, Egyptian, and even Assyrian folklore, there are the stories of a great beast that guards the entrance to Lebanon, deep in the forest." Shullat said. Enkidu stood and stared off into the distance. Something about what Shullat just said jogged a memory deep in his brain.

"What did you just say?" asked Enkidu.

"Now you are interested?" Shullat replied, throwing his arms up. "Frankly, I can never tell, what with you pacing the floor like an animal day and night. I wasn't sure you were even really listening!"

"Just tell me about this Guardian of the Cedar Forest!" Enkidu said, leaping over to where Shullat was standing. It took him by surprise, and he fell over backward onto his backside. "What is the name of this creature?" Shullat slid backward on the floor to get some distance

225

between himself and Enkidu, and then he stood up and dusted himself off. "What is its name?!" Enkidu insisted.

"Humbaba," answered Shullat. Enkidu's expression changed from irritation to deep concern. Shullat had never seen him quite so worried before; he even looked scared! Enkidu whispered the name again to himself as he began to pace the floor again, slowly. Then, he turned and looked at Shullat.

"Do not ever mention the idea to Gilgamesh!" Enkidu asked Shullat. He was taken aback at the firmness in Enkidu's voice.

"You can't order me what to do Enkidu!" Shullat shot back. "I am the Top General of the King's army, and if I want to inform the King about something, it is my right!" Enkidu approached Shullat, who, despite his bravery a second before, began to back up cautiously.

"You don't understand Shullat," Enkidu said to him, "I know that Gilgamesh will be too ambitious not to take on the challenge of conquering the Cedar Forest. If he does, he will surely die!"

"Gilgamesh? The King die?! Are you mad? I don't know if you've forgotten, but he is a God! Besides that, he defeated *you* in battle just a few months ago, or don't you remember?"

"I know what he is!" Enkidu shouted back angrily. Shullat took a few more steps back. Truth be told, he was very afraid of Enkidu when he was angry. Shullat tried to leave the room, but Enkidu jumped from one side of the room to the other, and in front of the doorway. He grabbed Shullat and lifted him off the ground easily. "You have no idea what you are fooling with! If Gilgamesh thought I was a hill to climb, then Humbaba is a mountain! Even with all of Gilgamesh's strength, he cannot defeat Humbaba. It is impossible for any man!"

"But..."Shullat began.

"His *is* still a man Shullat!" Enkidu said, cutting him off. "He may have enormous strength and power from the Gods, but he is still part man! And Humbaba *will* kill him! And for what? To have the wealth of the Cedar Forest? Is not Sumeria the most prosperous and mighty empire in the entire world already! What more do the Sumerians and its King need?"

Enkidu put down Shullat, who sighed in relief. He put his arm around Shullat, and spoke calmly, trying to reason with him. "Please Shullat; do not tell Gilgamesh what Sargon is doing. Surely Sargon will fail anyway; but I do not want Gilgamesh to even conceive of this idea to fight Humbaba and control the Cedar Forest. Promise me General."

"I will not tell Gilgamesh about Sargon," Shullat said weakly, putting his head down. "May I go now?"

"Yes, of course," Enkidu said, patting his shoulder. Shullat scuffled off, and Enkidu walked slowly back over to the window. He looked out at the splendor of the city below. There was sadness in his heart though. In spite of what he had just warned to Shullat, he knew that he would tell Gilgamesh; and he knew that Gilgamesh would want to conquer the forest. Nothing good could come out of it, Enkidu said to himself. He shook his head and waited for the inevitable to happen.

-----------------------------------------------------------

The men were scant and few. Most of them decided it was suicide to attempt it; but there were a select few who were brave enough to follow him anywhere. They believed in him, when others didn't. The other few men who were left after the last uprising had given up hope of ever defeating Gilgamesh. He was too powerful and well armed; not to mention he was a deity! But this new leader gave many of them hope again, though most thought he was a lunatic for even suggesting what he was suggesting!

Sargon walked among the men who had decided to go with him to the Cedar Forest of Lebanon. They were all lined up in front of him, armed with whatever few weapons they could find. There was no armor, as

Gilgamesh had confiscated everything they had, and as of late, their relations with the Egyptians weren't as close as it had been. Khasekemwy was preoccupied with building his own empire to care about the Assyrians anymore, so the weapons and supplies they used to receive from them were now nonexistent.

As Sargon walked past each of the men and patted them on the back, one of the other men who were crowded behind the line began to shout at him.

"You are a fool Sargon," the man yelled at him. "Even if you somehow conquer the Cedar Forest, we will never match the strength of Gilgamesh's army." Sargon stopped what he was doing and walked over to the man. The man turned his back on Sargon, and began to speak to the crowd behind him. "Gilgamesh is a changed man, I have seen it. Ever since his battle with the stranger from the northern forest, he has become a benevolent ruler." Then the man turned back to face Sargon. "We are all tired of fighting; and dying. Let us make peace and live under Sumerian rule again. It is a better life for us all." Another man standing next to him began to yell in agreement.

"What is your name?" Sargon asked the man.

"My name is Chori," he told Sargon. Sargon put his hand on Chori's soldier and began to nod his head in agreement. A smile came over Chori's face for a moment, but just a moment. With one quick move, Sargon plunged a small knife into Chori's belly. He fell over and writhed in pain as the blood pooled next to his body. Sargon waited a moment for Chori to die, then took his knife from his stomach. He wiped the blood from it, and then walked over to the other man who had been standing next to Chori. The other man tried to run away, but the other people in the crowd grabbed him by the arms and turned him to face Sargon.

"Please impart a message to the King for me," he told the man, holding the knife up to his cheek. The man quivered in fright, then lost control of his bowels. Sargon looked down, and then raised his head with a maniacal grin on his face. He played with the knife on the man's cheek as he spoke some more. "Tell Gilgamesh, that if he wishes to send spies among our people…." Sargon stopped a moment, and then slit the man's cheek in half. The man cried out in horrific pain as blood squirted from his wound. The other men behind him held him firm as he struggled to get free. Sargon put the blade up to the other cheek of the spy. "Tell him that he should be a little more careful who he sends…..lest they wind up like you." With that, Sargon slit the other man's cheek. He screamed in agony as the men who were holding him let him go. He fell to the ground and clutched at his face. The blood covered his hands and was oozing onto the ground.

Sargon looked at the men who had been holding him and nodded his head. One of them brought out a small sack. His name was Ashur. He reached into the sack and grabbed a handful of a white grainy substance. Sargon nodded his approval, and then two other men grabbed the traitor and held him up again. Sargon came over to the spy with the man holding the sack right behind him. Sargon lifted the man's head up with his hand and looked into his eyes.

"Don't get me wrong. I don't want you to die," Sargon told him. "I want you to live to tell the King what is waiting for him at our hands when we conquer the Cedar Forest." Sargon played with the white substance in his hand for a moment. "Now, this *will* hurt.....a lot!" Sargon told him, grinning. He looked over at Ashur and nodded, and then the two proceeded to rub the substance into the man's wounds. You could hear the scream of pain for a mile away as it burned into the man's face. The two men holding him let him go and he fell to the ground in a fetal position, screaming in agony.

"It's just salt, traitor," Ashur said, kicking him in the side. The spy spit up blood when he was struck. "It will heal your face so you will not get an infection. You will live long enough to return to Uruk." He began to walk away, then turned back and laughed, "Sorry about the side effects though. Knives can be a bit painful, and do leave nasty scars. Nothing we can do about that though!" He kicked the man again in the side for good measure, and then hurried up to catch up to Sargon who was walking away from the scene.

"What is troubling you Sargon?" Ashur asked him. Sargon stopped walking and looked over at his comrade.

"Do you really need to ask that?" he asked Ashur. Ashur laughed. "What is there not to worry about? We are living like dogs under Gilgamesh," Sargon continued. "Every time we mount an offensive, he smacks us down like gnats. And that was *with* the Egyptians' support. Now, without the Pharaoh's help, the battle is becoming ever more futile I fear."

"There is the Cedar Forest," he reminded Sargon. Sargon sighed and looked out toward the west.

"There is even less chance that we can defeat Humbaba," he huffed.

"Do you really believe in that children's fairy tale?" he asked Sargon.

"I do," he said with a serious expression. Ashur knew he wasn't joking. "But even if Humbaba doesn't exist, we will either have to fight the Lebanese army on their own land, or we will have to cross the many miles of dense forest, which is probably filled with wild animals, snakes, and who knows what other untold dangers?"

"But just think of the riches and power we would have if we succeed!" cried Ashur. Sargon let out a hollow laugh.

"I wonder how many others have had this same conversation?" he mused.

"We are different! We will succeed. I believe it!" Ashur boldly stated. Sargon looked at him and chuckled.

"Nothing scares you does it? But then again, why should it. You're size is greater than the Zagros Mountains combined!"

Ashur laughed. He was a huge man with dark skin. He stood nearly as tall as Gilgamesh, with a huge body of muscles. He had been one of Gilgamesh's stonecutters. Very few men could be one; it took enormous strength and endurance to do the job all day long in the blazing hot sun. The few who survived doing it wound up looking like Ashur, but many of the men died of heat exhaustion. He had fled many months ago, right before the last Assyrian attack. He had participated, but had been lucky enough to have escaped Gilgamesh when they had lost; that's when Sargon had showed up. He was from a small village in the north. He had neither a tall body, nor strong muscles, and wasn't a very handsome man. But the one thing he had was incredible charisma with the people. They trusted him, believed him, and looked to him for leadership. Sargon oozed natural leadership in his personality, and Ashur had been one of the first to recognize it and join him in forming a new army against the Sumerians. Sargon was very good at sizing up people, and he trusted Ashur, and made him his first lieutenant in their rag-tag army.

Some of Sargon's troops helped put the spy up on a donkey, and pointed it in the direction of Uruk. They gave the traitor a drink of water and then slapped the donkey on the backside to get it moving. The man slowly rode off into the distance, barely aware of anything going on.

"Do you think he will make it to Uruk?" Ashur asked Sargon amusedly. Sargon cocked his head and smiled, and then looked over at Ashur.

"Does it really matter?" he replied. Ashur and Sargon laughed and slapped each other on the back.

-------------------------------------------------------------

Enkidu was sitting out on the same dune that Gilgamesh often came to during sunset. He stared at the brilliant colors of the evening sun setting, when he heard footsteps approaching from afar. He knew them well. Enkidu sighed, and waited for the footsteps to grow closer.

"I was waiting for you," Enkidu said to Gilgamesh as he approached, without turning around. Gilgamesh stopped and smirked.

"How did you know I was behind you?" he queried. Enkidu laughed

"I do have the hearing of an animal, you know?" he said. Gilgamesh nodded his head, and then sat down beside him.

"The Kingdom is very prosperous since you and I have become friends, isn't it my friend," he said to Enkidu. Enkidu nodded his head. "And my subjects seem happier as well." Gilgamesh got up and started to pace back and forth. "But I have learned that in times of peace and prosperity to be the most worried......."

"I know why you are here," Enkidu said, interrupting. "You have had your conversation with Shullat, haven't you?" Enkidu turned and looked at Gilgamesh, who nodded his head slowly. "And I already know your decision."

"And what is that?" Gilgamesh asked. Enkidu stood up and turned to face his best friend.

"You *will* die Gilgamesh!" he warned him sternly. Gilgamesh turned his face away and looked out into the sunset.

"How can you be so sure?" he asked. Gilgamesh turned and looked Enkidu in the eyes. "How can you? I mean, have you ever even seen this Humbaba?" Enkidu shook his head. "Then how do we know if he even exists?" Gilgamesh asked. He came over and put his hand on Enkidu's shoulder. "Listen old friend, the rewards outweigh the risks. You have the luxury of living your life without concern for an entire Kingdom of people."

"I care about Uruk as much as you do, that is why I am here!" Enkidu balked.

"Yes, but it is *my* responsibility. I am the King! And I cannot go about my business without worrying about the enemies we have on all sides: the Egyptians, the Assyrians, and even the small bands of Akkadian clans that live in the south. Taking control of the Cedar Forest would ensure our dominance for a century to come!"

"I know all of this," Enkidu assured Gilgamesh. "But I also know that Humbaba is real. It is true that I have never encountered him, but I know of him; all of the animals know of him. Even though we do not speak with our tongues, we can still communicate in ways humans do not understand. I know of the Guardian of the Cedar Forest, and I know the images in my head do not lie!"

"And what are the images in your head?" asked Gilgamesh. Enkidu's expression changed to one of grave concern.

"He is the most powerful creature in this world Gilgamesh," he told him flatly. "Neither you nor I could ever hope to match his strength. He was made by the Gods to protect the entrance to Lebanon because the Lebanese people hold favor with them. No man, not even you, can defeat him! Not even with your entire army of men at your side!"

Gilgamesh put his hand up to his face and rubbed his chin. He was clearly thinking about what he had just been told. Then he looked at Enkidu and smiled.

"I don't need an army," he proclaimed to Enkidu. Enkidu looked at him with a blank look on his face, confused at his statement. "After all....." Gilgamesh continued, "I have you." Enkidu stared at Gilgamesh, who continued with his train of thought. "You said that I don't have the strength to beat him, and that may be true. But what about the strength of us combined? We are the two most powerful humans in the entire world. Surely, together, we can beat Humbaba!"

Enkidu looked at Gilgamesh a moment, and then fixed his gaze on the sunset. The deep red and purple colors were starting to fade; so was his hope of convincing Gilgamesh otherwise. Enkidu sat in silence as he thought for a moment about their situation. After a few minutes, he looked at Gilgamesh and then begrudgingly nodded his head.

"I suppose you are going with or without me," Enkidu said to Gilgamesh. The King nodded his head and smiled. "Well, you will need me if you have *any* chance of surviving." Gilgamesh patted Enkidu's back, and Enkidu stared out at the night sky again. "Anyway, I can't let my best friend go on his greatest adventure alone, can I?"

Gilgamesh and Enkidu both laughed and embraced one another. They walked back to the Palace as the reddish and purple colors of the sunset started to give way to the darkness of night. The stars shone brightly over Uruk, as if the Gods themselves were lighting the sky for them. Enkidu and Gilgamesh both hoped they would be watching over them as they faced Humbaba.

Enkidu was not mistaken about Humbaba. Utu, the Sun God has personally created Humbaba as a barrier between humans and the Cedar Forest of Lebanon. The Cedar Forest was ripe with resources, not just the much sought after Cedar wood that was used in building. Enlil, the God of the Sky, and his brother Enki, the God of the Sea and Wisdom, knew very well that any group of people who controlled the entire Cedar Forest would rule the world! Even the Lebanese, though they carried the favor of the Gods for their righteousness and servitude, were only allowed to take from the outer trees of the West side of the Forest. It was enough to sustain their economy, but not enough to make them a dominate power.

In the past, many groups of people had tried to enter the Cedar Forest, but all of them had disappeared, suffering horrible deaths. In recent years, the Cedar Forest and the story of Humbaba had been referred to by the people of Sumeria and Egypt as nothing more than a myth, as the two great powers had lost interest in even trying to conquer the unconquerable. But nothing was unconquerable to Gilgamesh in his mind. His bull-headed arrogance was rearing its ugly head once again, and this time, not even Enkidu could stop him from walking into facing the very fires of Hell itself.

Nininsina looked down on Gilgamesh from the sky above. She knew that the spiritual judges of the nether world, the Annunaki, were waiting for Gilgamesh's soul. They had craved it from the first breath that Gilgamesh had taken in the human world, and Humbaba might just be the one to finally deliver it to them on a silver platter! She looked down on her Son this night and wept in her heart. As she did, it began to rain over all Sumeria. She was no longer able to protect him and be by his side as she once did in her mortal body. His fate was in the hands of Anu now. She hoped that Enkidu would serve as his protector as he foolishly took on the Son of Utu for the ultimate human prize; the Cedar Forest.

-----------------------------------------------------------

It had been several months since Adad had last seen his guests. He hoped they were all right. Though he had witnessed what Enkidu could do, he has serious doubts that Gilgamesh could be defeated. Adad had seen with his own eyes the King defeat dozens of soldiers at a time, so he was less than certain that Enkidu could have defeated him. In fact, he assumed he had probably failed. There had been no word from Uruk, as Shamhat and Enkidu promised if they were victorious.

Day after day he sat alone in his small shack. There were a few other older farmers and fishermen that came to visit once in a moon, but mostly he was left to himself. None of them carried any news about any of the happenings in Uruk either. After the pair had left, there was no one to tend to the fields, so his crop had been greatly diminished. Adad was no longer physically able to run the farm by himself; he had been barely able to run things when Agga had been there to help him! All he could do was tend to a small garden, which grew just enough food to keep him alive. Once a month he made the trip out to the Caspian Sea to fetch some water on his donkey. Even his donkey had become ragged and tired without proper nutrition, and Adad feared he would die any day now.

To make matters worse, he had caught something recently. Something that made him periodically vomit up blood. He felt tired all the time, and his bones ached. He wasn't sure what it was, or how he got it, but whatever it was, it was taking its toll on him. Perhaps he was just old, he thought to himself. Shamhat had nursed him back to health when he had gone a bit mad after Agga's death, and Enkidu's discovery, but now that little bit of health had faded again. Most days he just sat in the same corner he had when the two were there, and let his mind wander. There were so many regrets he had. Things he should have done differently when he had fled Uruk. He missed his wife. Moreover, he missed his Son Agga. After his mother had died, they were all each other had for so many years.

And then there was the other matter. Adad wasn't sure, but he thought he may have sputtered something about it out to Shamhat and Enkidu when he had been less than aware of what was going on. In any case, the memory of what happened still haunted him; even after 16 years, he could still vividly recall the events of that day. Every sight, every smell, every action; the blazing fire, and every cry for help and horrific last gasp for breath he had heard! A tear began to roll down Adad's cheek as he sat and thought. How could he have left her behind? It was inconceivable now. He had been so worried for her safety though. They were coming for him that day, and they would kill every member of his family in the process. They had already killed his wife! What was he to do then?

Adad put his head between his knees and began to weep. He shook his head and let the tears flow freely from his eyes. Who cared anymore anyway, he thought? There was no one left to be ashamed in front of. It was only him; him and his guilt. It was poor company. Just then, he began to cough. Blood came up out from his mouth. It was getting worse, his condition. He knew that he had very little time left to live. Adad sat on the floor and looked out the small window of his run-down shack. He looked out at the sky and prayed to Anu. He prayed that he would not die before the truth was known; it had to be known. He could not die before all was set right, and he was allowed to see her one more time; just once more, he prayed to Anu! His soul could not move on in peace without it.

Getting out a piece of stone tablet, he began to carve writing on it. Adad coughed and wheezed as he wrote, but he did not stop, not even for a drink of water. He was determined to tell the truth, and if he were to die before he made it to Uruk to see his brother, he wanted there to be a record of what had happened that day. If Anu were kind enough, he would let her see the tablet if he died on the way. Then she would finally know what happened all those years ago; and she would know how much he loved her and missed her all those years! Maybe she would understand and forgive him, and maybe not. It didn't matter now. His time on Earth was coming to an end, and he had to set things right!

After many days, Adad had finished his testimonial. He packed the stone tablets, some vegetables and fruit he had grown, and a clay jar of water onto his donkey. It was all he had left in the house. He didn't care though. The old man had no intention of coming back. Adad struggled to get up on the broken down ass, but he finally made it, huffing and coughing all the time. With a weak kick, the donkey headed off in the direction of Uruk; and his brother. He was the only one alive who knew what Adad knew. Adad hoped he was still alive himself, or her for that matter. The blazing sun overhead mocked him, as he rode off toward the King's city. It would be a few days trip, and he wasn't sure if he would survive the desert. But it didn't really matter now anyway, Adad said to himself; he had been dead for 16 years already!

--------------------------------------------------------------

Delondra waited until nightfall to sneak out of her Cousin's house. After the horrible vision she had seen during her episode the month before, she could no longer even sleep without having nightmares about it. Small parts of the vision replayed over and over in her sleep every night. She often woke up drenched in sweat and breathing heavily. When Siduri or Irkalla would come to her room, she would say it was nothing. Both of them had grown very concerned for her over the past weeks. It seemed every night she was having bad dreams. She barely ate, and spent much of her time wandering aimlessly around the town. Irkalla suggested that it may be time that they themselves seeked the help of an Ashipu as her parents had. Siduri reminded her it did little good the last time.

The vision she kept having was of Gilgamesh and another man in a dark forest. She wasn't sure where, but there was no light except for the glow of fire around them. The other man was tall like Gilgamesh and had long shaggy hair on his head and body. Then, something came at them; something huge and menacing. It towered over both of the men and struck them both with incredible force. There was blood everywhere and fire surrounding the two men. There were shouts and groans of pain and suffering. There was a terrifying cackle from the thing that attacked them. That was all she had seen. Many times since she had tried to force the vision back in her mind so she could see more about what it was Gilgamesh and this other man would face, but it was no use; it just didn't work that way. She couldn't control when the visions would happen, but they always seemed to come true, and the ones that came during her seizures were more graphic and detailed than the other quick flashes of the future she frequently experienced. When she had returned to the Palace for her last month of service, she had met Enkidu for the first time. Little did she know, though, she had already seen him before. *He* was the other man in her vision with Gilgamesh! When she realized it, she was even more convinced of the truth to what she had just seen not long ago in her seizure state.

As quietly as she could, she snuck out the front of the house, and out to where the horses were kept. The people of Kish, though it was not as rich as it had been when it had been the seat of power for the region, were still wealthy, and the middle-class people mostly rode horses, and not donkeys like the lower class. It was fortunate for Delondra too, because she had no hope of ever reaching them before they left if she were riding a donkey.

Delondra had gotten wind that the two were setting off to the Cedar Forest the next morning from one of the townspeople. She had decided then that she had to go and warn the two of what she saw. She had never told the King or Enkidu of her visions when she was at the palace, fearing she would be discarded as a crazy person. Crazy people in Uruk were often put in isolation, much like prisoners.

It was no longer her place to even enter the Palace anymore as she didn't belong to the harem, but she had to try. Delondra wasn't so concerned for Gilgamesh. Though he had changed his ways considerably, the stings of his past deeds were still fresh in her mind. No, her concern was for another. It was for Enkidu. Delondra had to admit that she had found herself attracted to him as soon as they had met. As the month had gone by, she had the opportunity to spend a lot of time with Enkidu. He mostly liked to keep his own company because he was still feeling a little out of place around people, but after awhile, Enkidu had grown to enjoy her company. Maybe because she was a little odd herself; many people shunned her because of her strange demeanor, wispy voice, and interesting way of looking at the world.

Delondra had never found anyone to be as genuine as Enkidu, and she had quickly fallen for him, though she had not yet told him. She suspected he knew though, because she hung on his arm most of the day like a puppy with its master. It had killed her to leave after she turned 18, but she had to. It was the law. Delondra had tried to persuade Gilgamesh to give her another duty, any duty in the palace, so she could stay. He had declined.

Now, she was headed off to Uruk again. She had to warn Enkidu, if she could. Delondra had not told Siduri or Irkalla that she was leaving, or of what she had seen that day. She knew they wouldn't believe her, and they would try to prevent her from going for her own good. Delondra knew they would be upset and very worried when they found her missing, but she *had* to go. She knew she risked many things by going, but she didn't care.

Delondra rode as fast as she could toward Uruk. Her heart raced and cheeks flushed as she thought of Enkidu, and the prospect of seeing him again. A huge smile came over her face as she rode along in the coolness of the night, the stars hanging over her head. She looked up at them as she rode with breakneck speed, pushing her horse to reach the city by morning. She knew that if she were to arrive too late, they would have already gone, and she might never see Enkidu again. It wasn't something she wanted to think about. She kicked her horse's side again and rode toward the great city.

Suddenly, something caught her attention out of the corner of her eye. It looked like fire. She brought her horse to a halt and stared off into the distance. It did look like a campfire. But what would people be doing out here, in the middle of nowhere, she thought to herself? The path from Kish to Uruk had nothing in between; just desert and flat land. Sure enough, though, as she rode toward the dancing light, it was clearly a small camp that someone had set up. There was no person in sight, nor a horse or donkey. A few things were lying on the ground: a small mat for sitting, a small knife, a clay water flask, and a few fruits.

Something told her she shouldn't come any closer, but she felt compelled by her curiosity to see if someone was there. Slowly she rode her horse over toward the fire. The still of the night and lack of any movement began to bother her. It seemed too calm and quiet. Delondra's heart began to beat harder and faster. She looked from side to side in case anyone was there, but found no one.

When she reached the camp, there was still not a soul who had come out of the darkness to meet her. It was as if someone was there just a moment ago, then abandoned the site, without even enough time to put out the fire they had started. Something about the whole situation just didn't seem right to Delondra. She turned her horse around and began to ride away from the camp. Suddenly, something came out of nowhere and hit her. Delondra fell off her horse and onto the cold sand on the ground below. Her head ached as she writhed on the ground in pain. She had no idea what hit her, but it was hard! It almost felt like a rock or something. She grabbed her arm and cried out in pain. Tears flowed from her eyes as she sat up in the sand and looked down at her wound. Whatever it was had hit her on her left arm and cut her open badly. She wiggled her hand, but it had begun to lose its feeling. Delondra pulled away the hand that had been clutching her hurt arm and saw something red. It was blood, and it was pouring out of her quickly. Her eyes grew wide. She began to panic and hyperventilate. Everything around her began to swirl, and she felt dizzy. She fell back onto the sand. That was the last thing she recalled.

As she began to regain consciousness, she could see two blurry figures standing above her. One was a large, dark-skinned man who was bald; the other was a short man with long hair that went halfway down his back. He was pacing back and forth; he looked frantic.

"I didn't know it was a woman!" the large man said to the smaller one. The small man continued pacing back and forth and periodically looking down at Delondra.

"You couldn't tell the shape of a woman from a man?" he asked the large fellow. The large man shrugged his shoulders. "I hope she isn't dead!"

"I don't think so. I think she just passed out from the pain," the large man said. The smaller man with the long hair kneeled down by Delondra's side. He put his hand on her forehead and felt to make sure she was still warm. They had layed her body by the fire to make sure she kept warm as the night air had become chilly. The small one had bandaged the wound in Delondra's arm with a piece of cloth, and had tied it tight to stop the bleeding.

The large man had left the campsite for only a moment because he thought he had seen a rabbit nearby, and wanted to catch it for dinner. The other one had been out patrolling the small campsite in a 100 meter circumference around it, making sure nobody would find them there.

A few nights before, Sargon had decided that a trip to the Cedar Forest would be too risky for their small army to undertake. They would surely perish at the hands of Humbaba, or the Lebanese army for that matter. Sargon had finally decided that he could not defeat Gilgamesh with any type for force; instead, he would have to use his wits to beat him. His new plan was to pose as a Sumerian, and try to gain access within the walls of Uruk. He believed he could pass for one, because his grandfather had been from Sumeria, and there were a few Sumerian traits in his face. It was actually hard to tell exactly where Sargon was from, something he found to be a blessing, as it allowed him to blend in wherever he went. Sargon had mastered many languages as well, so he could pass for nearly any race. He had learned early in his life from his mother that he must always be one step ahead of everyone, and that persuasion and manipulation were often more powerful tools than any weapon.

Once inside Uruk, Sargon and Ashur would move freely about, spying on their infrastructure; looking for weaknesses in their wall. Watching how the Sumerian army trained for battle. Sargon knew that Gilgamesh already knew of his desire to take the cedar forest, and was certain that the King would want to stop him; or take the forest for himself. Either way, the champion of Uruk would be gone, and with the knowledge that Sargon would return with to his Assyrian following, maybe he could mount an offensive. Or for that matter, he could use his manipulative skills to bring dissension in the ranks of Gilgamesh's army; anything to give himself and the Assyrians the upper hand while Gilgamesh was preoccupied with Lebanon.

Delondra began to move her head and arms as she came back to life. She had nearly died from the loss of blood when Ashur had thrown the large rock, which was intended for her head actually. It had hit her in the arm instead, knocking her off the horse. It was one of Ashur's talents, being able to throw rocks and hard objects using a piece of long cloth. He would place the rock in the cloth, and then he would twirl it in the air as fast as he could. Then he would let go the rock that was inside the cloth, and hit whatever target he aimed at. It was a makeshift weapon for someone who had none, but he had become very proficient over the years in being able to hit a target from up to 200 feet away. On this occasion, he had thought that Delondra was perhaps a patrol guard or someone from Uruk, and they might discover that they were there before Sargon wanted to be known.

"I'm sorry about my friend," Sargon said to Delondra, kneeling down beside her and putting his hand on her head. "He thought you were an enemy." Delondra didn't answer. She was still too groggy.

"Lucky I didn't hit your head or you wouldn't be alive right now," Ashur told her in his deep booming voice. Delondra was confused and a bit unnerved by these two strangers. Who were these people anyway? And what were they doing out here?

"What's your name?" Sargon asked in the kindest and gentlest voice he could. He took Delondra's hand and helped her to sit up. She grabbed at her arm because of the pain, but Sargon caught her hand and guided it back down to her lap. "Don't want to do that now," he told her. "It's just starting to heal, and you don't want to rip it open again, do you?"

"Who are you?" Delondra said weakly to Sargon. He smiled at her and introduced himself.

"I am Hanash, and this is my friend Kur. We are from a small village just outside of Ninevah, in the North."

"You are fishermen?" Delondra asked.

"Why do you ask?" Sargon responded.

"It's just that most of the people from Ninevah are known to be fishermen, not much else. I'm sorry; I didn't mean to offend you if you are not."

"Not at all," Sargon said, waving his hand. "Why are you out in the middle of the desert at night my dear girl?"

"I was on my way to Uruk to see the King," she told him. Sargon's eyes grew wide.

"Really. Why were you doing that?" he asked.

"I.....well......I can't tell you that," Delondra replied. She felt a little uncomfortable with answering questions from this strange man. "How is it that you are this far away from Ninevah?" Ashur looked at Sargon, waiting for the story he would come up with.

"Well," he began, sitting down beside her, "it just so happens that we are also on our way to see the King."

"The two of you from Ninevah are off to see the King?" she asked skeptically.

"Why is this so strange?" Sargon inquired.

"People from Ninevah are well known to hate Gilgamesh," she proclaimed. "Furthermore, there hasn't been a person from Ninevah or any of the outlying regions of Sumeria that has been to Uruk since before Dumuzi took power, because of the disagreements on what God to worship!" Delondra said, not even stopping to take a breath. As she waited for an answer, Ashur began to pace back and forth nervously. He didn't want to have to kill this girl, but she was becoming entirely too suspicious of them!

"Well, you see my dear girl," Sargon began without skipping a beat, "I'm sorry, what was your name?"

"Delondra," she replied.

"Well, Delondra, you are right that we are but simple fishermen. Frankly, I personally don't know much about Gods and so forth. We are simple people who live life one day at a time and hope there is enough bounty of fish and grains to keep us alive. In fact, it is a misconception that Ninevites are so against the King. This is a little lie made up by the Assyrians, who hope to persuade the northern territories to rebel with them.....Anyway, I got a bit off track, didn't I? We came down here to beg the King to send help to Ninevah."

"Help? Why do you need help?" Delondra asked. Sargon looked up at Ashur. Ashur turned and continued pacing back and forth. He wondered what brilliant thing Sargon would say next!

"Well.....you see......" Sargon was searching for words, but they failed him in this moment. Usually he could come up with any kind of cover story for his real intentions, but he was finding it hard to find something in his mind that would satisfy this girl's curiosity. She was obviously very intelligent. He finally looked over at Ashur and threw up his hands. "Alright my dear, you caught us red-handed!"

"What do you mean?" Delondra asked, standing to her feet with a bit of alarm. Sargon stood up with her and bowed.

"Please forgive me trying to fool an intelligent girl such as you." Sargon stood back upright and continued. "We are actually from Lagash, not far east from here. But then, you probably knew that, didn't you? I mean, what Ninevite could speak so well, after all."

"Yes, it's true," Delondra answered. "You are from Lagash, you say? I know it well."

"Well, you have to know then that, well, frankly we don't approve very much of Gilgamesh."

"I know this. It is the same in Kish and many places these days," she said.

"Exactly," Sargon said. "However, despite that, we have come to warn the King about an impending danger to the Kingdom."

"Danger? What danger?" Delondra asked.

Sargon looked over at Ashur, and then continued, "We have come to learn of a plot by the Assyrians to travel to the Cedar Forest." Ashur stared over at Sargon. He hadn't expected him to tell her this.

"How did you come by this information.....Hanash, is it?"

"Yes, Hanash is my name. Anyway, we came upon an Assyrian while we were out tending our field. He was delirious, and wandering about. Being that he *was* still a human being, even if he was an Assyrian, my friend and I gave him fresh clothes and fed him. After he had regained a bit of his senses, he told us his name was Ashur, and that he had been part of the rebellion a few months back that had lost to the King. Apparently, they have a new leader, and this new leader, Sargon I think it was, was going to lead a mission to the Cedar Forest hoping to capture its wealth. Wealth he hoped would be enough to unseat Uruk and Gilgamesh as supreme ruler."

Delondra looked at Sargon as he told the story. Never once did he flinch or bat a nervous eye. He told it quite convincingly actually.

"Why didn't you just tell me that in the first place," she asked Sargon. He looked down and shrugged his shoulders.

"It's a little hard to believe, I admit. The whole story sounds made up or something and you might have got the impression that we were out here up to no good." Then Sargon looked directly into Delondra's eyes. "But I swear it's the truth, on the life of my dear mother." Ashur turned away from Sargon and Delondra, as he chuckled under his breath. Sargon's mother was long dead, and besides that, they had had a falling out before she died. In actuality, she hated her only son for being so manipulative, even if she was the one who taught him to be so!

Delondra looked into his eyes for a moment, and then seemed satisfied. "Why don't you and your friend.....I'm sorry, what was your name again?" Ashur looked over at Sargon with a bewildered look as he couldn't remember.

"Kur. His name is Kur, but he doesn't speak. He's a mute," Sargon said. Ashur gave Sargon an angry look, but he shrugged it off.

"Why don't you and Kur accompany me to Uruk? I could surely use the company. Besides, I am still a bit weak and could use your help. I need to get to Uruk as fast as possible, but I don't think I have the strength now to ride."

"You are quite right my dear girl," Sargon told her with a smile. He looked over at Ashur, who was shaking his head and chuckling to himself. He was quite the salesman, Ashur whispered to himself.

"Besides which, I'm afraid your horse has run off, but you are welcome to ride with me," Sargon told her. Delondra nodded her head, not having much other choice. "I will make sure you get where you are going in time!"

Sargon packed up his supplies and packed them on the horse. After hopping up onto the animal, he held out his hand for Delondra. She tried to take it, but she was still in great pain because of her wound. Ashur came over and grabbed her waist, then lifted her up on the horse with ease, and placed her in back of Sargon. Ashur then mounted his own horse, and the three rode toward Uruk to see the King.

Sargon wiped his head off. It was full of sweat, even though it was chilly out. He hoped she didn't notice how nervous he actually was trying to persuade her of their innocence of any wrongdoing. In any case, it must have worked, or she wouldn't be traveling with them now. And she would be very useful in helping them get into Uruk to see Gilgamesh, and helping convince him they were who they said they were; Hanish and Kur from Lagash.

---------------------------------------------------------

Gilgamesh had wanted to keep their plans to travel to the Cedar Forest secret, so as not to alarm the people of Uruk, or the Elder Council. Enkidu had persuaded Gilgamesh to appoint this elder council after their epic duel. He felt that it would help instill trust in the King by giving representatives of the people a voice in the political scheme. Gilgamesh had vehemently rejected the idea in the beginning, but was then persuaded later to do it. It consisted of five men, all over the age of 40, from differing sections of Uruk. Gilgamesh knew that he would *have* to tell them before he left, but he was putting it off as long as he could.

When they had informed the Elder council of what they were about to do, they had thought the two of them mad! It was inconceivable that anyone would believe in the "fairy tale" of Humbaba anymore, or that anyone should venture that far out, and near Egyptian and Assyrian land. All this just to get to the Cedar Forest, where they would probably surely die at the hands of the Lebanese army! Gilgamesh had pleaded his case, and despite the grumblings of the council, they had finally acquiesced, and gave their blessing. It hardly mattered though, as Gilgamesh would have gone anyway. There was no one to stop him after all. After their stern warnings about being careful and so on, the two set out for Lebanon. It was a monumental undertaking, and Gilgamesh knew it. Even if they reached the Cedar Forest and somehow conquered Humbaba, not to mention the other perils of the forest, and the Assyrians or Egyptians they might meet along the way, it wasn't clear how he would transport the mighty cedar trees back to Uruk. Gilgamesh thought it best not to over think the details, and he and Enkidu headed out on their great adventure.

Early the next morning, Gilgamesh and Enkidu hopped up on their horses, and began their long journey to the Cedar Forest. They would have to be careful not to cross into Egyptian territory. To do this, they would have to travel in a roundabout manner, first going north, and then cutting across to the West. This would put them in Assyrian territory, but it was far more desirable to be faced with Assyrians than Egyptians.

Both of them were leading another horse by a rope. In total, there were four horses, two for each of them; one to ride, and one to carry the weeks of supplies they would need of food and water. Mostly it was for Gilgamesh though. Enkidu was endowed with the ability to go without food and water for very long periods if he needed to, but Gilgamesh, though he was half God, needed to eat and drink as a normal man. Despite his great strength, Gilgamesh was still limited by the same weakness as ordinary men, a fact that had always bothered him.

A crowd had gathered to see them off. Enkidu looked around to see if Delondra was there among the crowd of people who had gathered around them to see them off. He couldn't find her. Then he remembered that she had been released and gone back home. For Enkidu, weeks often passed before he noticed anything to do with the other people of the Palace. He was always off in another world in his mind, perhaps habit from when he was more like an animal. Sometimes he had problems focusing on conversation and such, but when he did, he spoke like a poet with very profound thoughts. He did like Delondra though, and had found her company quite pleasant and satisfying. Enkidu was sad to remember that she had left and he wouldn't be able to say goodbye as they left for Lebanon.

Gilgamesh waved to his subjects, then reared his horse and rode off toward the city gate. Enkidu followed suit. The people cheered as they left, though it wasn't entirely clear that they meant it, or were still a little afraid of Gilgamesh's wrath. Some of the cheers seemed half-hearted. Shullat stood with his spear in one hand and sword in the other, and watched the two men leave. He silently prayed a prayer to Anu, the father of the Gods that they may be safe.

While they were away, he was left to be in charge of the Kingdom. Gilgamesh felt he could trust no other. Shullat hoped to prove him right, but he was worried. If word got out to Pharaoh Khasekemwy that Gilgamesh was on this fool-hardy mission, he may attack him en route; or he may attack Uruk without its two strongest warriors to protect them. His Egyptian spies had been more fortunate than the one who had returned a day earlier from Assyria. He had been permanently scarred by this new Assyrian leader, Sargon. The Assyrians had found out about the spies, but thus far, the Egyptian operatives still remained in secret; at least he hoped!

The spies in Egypt had told Shullat that the size of the Egyptian army had grown exponentially. Khasekemwy had a way with persuading his subjects to rally behind his efforts to go to war with Gilgamesh for the good of the Egyptian Empire. Khasekemwy implored his people that they needed to strike before Gilgamesh did. Also, their trade with the Assyrians, Akkadians, and even the Lebanese was growing. It would be hard for the Sumerians and Gilgamesh to compete if this kept up much longer.

Shullat watched as the two warriors faded off into the distance. The people of Uruk dispersed and went back to their homes. Shullat walked up to Gilgamesh's favorite dune, and gazed out at the sky, hoping to find the same inspiration that the King did each night as he stood there and gazed at the horizon. He hoped that Enkidu and Gilgamesh would be victorious. It may very well mean that the survival of the Sumerian empire depended on it.

Shullat let out a sigh and stroked his beard. He truly hoped that the Egyptians would not attack before Gilgamesh and Enkidu returned. If they did attack, Shullat thought to himself.....well, then he only prayed that the Gods would show mercy to the King's city and the people of Sumeria!